THE INTIMATE MEMOIRS OF
AN EDWARDIAN DANDY
Volume III

Also in this series

THE INTIMATE MEMOIRS OF
AN EDWARDIAN DANDY
Volume I

THE INTIMATE MEMOIRS OF
AN EDWARDIAN DANDY
Volume II

THE INTIMATE MEMOIRS OF
AN EDWARDIAN DANDY
Volume IV

The Intimate Memoirs of an Edwardian Dandy

Volume III
Art For Art's Sake

Rupert Mountjoy

Edited and Introduced by
PROFESSOR ALEXANDER RASPIS

WARNER BOOKS

A *Warner* Book

First published in Great Britain in 1993
by Warner Books
Reprinted 1994

Copyright © Potiphar Productions 1993

The moral right of the author has been asserted.

*All characters in this publication are fictitious and
any resemblance to real persons, living or dead,
is purely coincidental.*

All rights reserved.
No part of this publication may be reproduced,
stored in a retrieval system or transmitted, in any
form or by any means, without the prior
permission in writing of the publisher, nor be
otherwise circulated in any form of binding or
cover other than that in which it is published and
without a similar condition including this
condition being imposed on the subsequent purchaser.

A CIP catalogue record for this book
is available from the British Library

ISBN 0 7515 0061 5

Photoset in North Wales by
Derek Doyle & Associates, Mold, Clwyd,
Printed in England by Clays Ltd, St Ives plc

Warner Books
A Division of
Little, Brown and Company (UK)
Brettenham House
Lancaster Place
London WC2E 7EN

This is for Barbara, John and especially Ray F.

Introduction

THE GLITTER OF RANK, WEALTH and fashion associated with the early years of the twentieth century were not confined to Great Britain. In Vienna, the glittering capital of the Austro-Hungarian Empire, the cavalry officers replete in their magnificent uniforms were waltzing the nights away and dining with their mistresses in discreet little supper-rooms; in America, the idiotic extravaganzas of the robber barons and their families made the headlines in the rapidly burgeoning popular press all over Europe and in Paris, the Left Bank seethed with many daring new artistic, social and philosophic ideas.

Yet without doubt it was the lives of the wealthy upper class English Edwardians, the heirs and custodians of an awe-inspiring Empire upon which the sun never set, that occupy centre stage during this so-called Golden Age when taxation was low, inflation unknown and masses of 'common' people were eager to be hired as domestic servants for absurdly small wages.

Of course, this colourful decade is too often viewed through nostalgic rose-tinted glasses. Living conditions for poor people were shocking, with at least one third of the population in the slums of London and other major cities, eking out a wretched existence below a decent level of subsistence. To quote the writer J.B. Priestley: 'They were overworked, underpaid and crowded into slum property that ought to have been pulled down years before . . . in London, the West End was already establishing "missions" in the East End, just as the Victorians had sent their missionaries to India, China, and darkest Africa.'

But for the idle, hedonistic rich, the years between the death of Queen Victoria and the Great War offered tremendous opportunities for enjoyment. These were aided by the rapid development of such luxuries as motor transport, the telephone and above all a monarch such as the extrovert Edward VII, who made little secret of his enjoyment of the pleasures of the flesh!

Rupert Mountjoy was a typical young man-about-town of these times with plenty of money and little inclination to work at anything except the diary which he began at the age of fifteen just before his initiation by the pretty daughter of a neighbour into the joys of sex. Since then, as he frankly admitted, his chief interest was in *l'art de faire l'amour*, which led to his pursuit (with no little success) of a never-ending number of the most ravishing and desirable girls in London.

And he had plenty of time to indulge himself, for though he was unquestionably possessed of a kindly, liberal disposition and attached much weight to the idea of *noblesse oblige*, he had little to occupy himself with in London except the pursuit of pleasure. For Rupert Mountjoy, this involved making love to a wide range of nubile females, from cheery young servants at home or in his friends' houses to the wild, fun-loving contemporaries of his own social class.

He was a member of the notorious Cremornites Club, a semi-secret fraternity of young rakes, and was a frequent visitor to the plush headquarters of the Club in Green Street, Mayfair, where King Edward VII is known to have brought his mistresses for discreet romps, often with such raffish companions as the Honourable Randolph Joynes, Sir Nicholas 'Mad Nick' Clee and Colonel Alan Brooke of the Household Cavalry.

As the distinguished social historian Dr Warwick Jackson drily noted in his foreword to the first book of Rupert's reminiscences, *The Intimate Memoirs Of An Edwardian Dandy Volume One: Youthful Scandals*, 'Rupert Mountjoy's lifestyle was hardly stressful! It consisted of huge luncheons after lazy morning recovering from the nights before, followed by unhurried afternoons spent leafing through the sporting magazines at the club, and the day was rounded off, perhaps, by a formal dinner party or by an evening at one of the popular West End theatres and afterwards, to complete matters, he and his cronies would visit one of the *maisons privées* to take their pick of the pretty girls available as bed-mates for the night.'

As his memoirs make clear, Rupert and his comrades left no stones unturned in their search for novel erotic entertainments. They threw themselves into London's night-life, shedding the shackles of convention as easily as they pulled off the garters of the saucy chorus girls who joined in the revels which took place behind closed doors but which were chronicled by Rupert in these uncensored, uninhibited memoirs.

We are fortunate that his extraordinarily explicit account of his day-to-day and night-by-night erotic escapades has survived for they were not originally written for public consumption. But in 1913 Rupert found himself frighteningly short of funds, after a huge row with his father and an unwise speculation involving the purchase of three racehorses, and was forced to bow to parental pressure and decamp to Australia.

But before he left London for Sydney he wrote to the family solicitor, Sir David Godfrey, asking him to sell his scribblings for the best possible price. Sir David was an adroit negotiator who had built up a thriving practice hushing up potential scandals and sorting out the often tangled affairs of cuckolded country gentlemen and indiscreet titled ladies, including several from the King's own charmed circle of friends. He was also himself a man of varied sexual proclivities and so had no qualms about selling Rupert's diaries to Max Dalmaine, the editor of the Cremornites quarterly journal in which they were serialised until the autumn of 1917. Few copies of these magazines have survived – but in 1990 an almost complete set of The Cremorne Dining Society Journal from 1913 to 1918 was discovered in a locked wooden cabinet during the refurbishment of an old water mill on the River Windrush in Oxfordshire and it is from these rescued pamphlets that this and other books in the series are taken.

A particularly interesting point of social history in this book concerns Rupert's involvement with an exhibition in London of pictures by among others, his first lover, the young Yorkshire artist Diana Wigmore, and some far more famous and distinguished French impressionists such as Cézanne, Matisse and Gauguin.

I believe that he was not over-exaggerating the furore caused by these paintings which the critics labelled as 'filthy and depraved', for at a famous exhibition in 1910 at the Grafton Galleries of modern foreign artists, Desmond MacCarthy recalled: 'Soon after ten the Press began to arrive. Now anything new in art is apt to provoke the same kind of indignation as immoral conduct and vice is detected in perfectly innocent pictures . . . anyhow, as I walked about the tittering newspaper critics busily taking notes I kept overhearing such remarks as "pure pornography", "admirably indecent" . . . and from the opening day the public flocked and the big rooms echoed with explosions of laughter and indignation . . .'

Similar explosions of gaiety and anger may well have been caused by the publication of Rupert's intimate diary; his robust vitality must have shocked even readers of The Cremorne Dining Society Journal. His lusty narrative, penned with an unselfconscious gusto, contains some of the frankest evocations and descriptions of a variety of sexual acts to be found in erotic writings of this era. Lovers of gallant literature will surely be delighted that Rupert's saucy narrative is once again available and this time to a far wider audience. Social historians too will also find much of interest, not least in Rupert and his contemporaries' fierce resistance to the suffocating, guilt-ridden and above all hypocritical moral climate of the time.

But above all, this novel is for the general broad-minded reader, as Louis Lombert commented in *His Mighty Engine* – a seminal study of turn of the century erotica: 'Copies of Rupert Mountjoy's memoirs have fortunately survived to delight and amuse, as well as providing us with an unusual and unconventional insight into the manners and *mores* of a vanished world.'

Alexander Raspis

Birmingham. January, 1993

'I am not over-fond of resisting temptation.'

William Beckford [1759-1844]: *Vathek*

CHAPTER ONE

A Menu To Savour

I WELL REMEMBER STANDING IN front of the fire in the drawing-room after breakfast on the morning of October 28 1905. Outside in Bedford Square the weather looked distinctly chilly and a brisk wind was winnowing the last big harvest of leaves from the trees. It was a good morning to stay indoors, I reflected, as a sudden squall briefly rattled the windows, though I would have to go out at about half past twelve, as I had accepted a luncheon invitation from a new acquaintance, Miss Nancy Carrington.

Of course, I could have always telephoned and pleaded that a trifling indisposition would prevent my presence at her table, but on the other hand, Miss Carrington only lived across the road and, even more important, she was a good-looking, young American lady from Boston whose wealthy family had rented a house for her in Bloomsbury to enable her to continue her studies in the nearby British Museum during the six months she planned to stay in London.

Nancy Carrington had called round last Thursday, which happened to be my twenty-second birthday, 'to meet my new English neighbours' and I had been very much taken by the sensual beauty of this lovely rose cheeked girl, whose long blonde hair cascaded down in ringlets to her shoulders and in whose bright blue eyes appeared a merry twinkle when she smiled. She had been wearing a figure hugging dress nipped in at the waist which accentuated not only her slender frame but also her pert, uptilted breasts which thrust saucily against an exquisitely fine silk blouse.

When, during the course of our conversation, I happened to mention that I was celebrating my birthday, she immediately invited me over to her house for a celebratory luncheon. At first I demurred, but she insisted, saying that her cook had just completed a *cordon bleu* course at Mrs Bickler's Academy of Domestic Science and that she would welcome the excuse to make a small party which would give her cook the chance to show off her newly learned prowess.

I rang the bell and my footman Edwards promptly appeared with a sheaf of letters on a silver salver. 'The second post has just arrived, sir,' he said, passing the tray to me. 'Thank you, Edwards, I'll read these in the library. Meanwhile, would you please telephone Harrods and ask them to deliver by noon a large bouquet of flowers suitable for a gentleman to take as a gift to a lady who has invited him for luncheon.'

'Certainly, sir,' said Edwards, bowing slightly. 'May I presume that the bouquet is for Miss Carrington at number forty-seven? If so, may I recommend chrysanthemums as the lady is particularly fond of them.'

It never fails to surprise me how servants glean their information but it is a fact that nothing went on at Albion Towers – our family home near the sleepy little Yorkshire village of Wharton – which was not known by Goldhill, our old butler, and his staff, and which was doubtless discussed in detail in the servants' hall! But in this case, as will shortly be shown, I soon found out how Edwards knew about Nancy Carrington's taste in flowers, it being the result of a romantic liaison my young footman had formed with Nancy's personal maid.

After telling Edwards that I would be dining at my club that evening, I went into the library to open the post. The first letter was from my tailor, Mr Rabinowitz, thanking me for the prompt payment I had made for my new suit and offering to make me an overcoat, at a very moderate cost, out of a beautiful eighteen ounce grey tweed cloth which he had bought directly from the mill. I filed the letter away for future reference and then opened the envelope postmarked Knaresborough which suggested that the letter inside came from my parents.

It was indeed a short note from my father, informing me that His Majesty King Edward VII would be visiting Yorkshire in three weeks time and that we had been invited to a reception in York on November 15 given in honour of the visit by the Deputy Lord Lieutenant of Yorkshire. Would I please let him know as soon as possible whether I wanted to attend? My mother had also scribbled a short note to add that our neighbours

Dr and Mrs Wigmore had also been invited and would attend as would their daughter Diana, the lovely girl who readers of my first book [*The Intimate Memoirs Of An Edwardian Dandy Volume One: Youthful Scandals* – Editor] will recall, was my guide and partner on that never to be forgotten summer's afternoon seven years before when I first sheathed my cock in a wet and welcoming cunney.

Whether wonderful or disastrous, one never forgets one's first fuck: I was a naïve schoolboy of fifteen and at first, frankly, bewildered by my maiden voyage along the highway of love; but I was fortunate enough to be shown the ropes by a sophisticated girl who took the trouble to explain how best I could please us both and thus cater for our joint needs. Diana is a talented artist and is working in Paris at present but whenever we see each other we usually end up in bed.

If for no other reason, this was a good enough bait to make me accept the invitation to go up to York, though I would probably have agreed to do so in any case, because I wanted to pay my respects to my old Uncle Humphrey who lived in Harrogate. It was Uncle Humphrey, my mother's eldest brother, who had persuaded my parents that I should spend a year sampling the delights of London after having gained (God knows how!) an upper second-class degree in law at Oxford University. [*For an explicit account of Rupert's hectic life at University read The Intimate Memoirs Of An Edwardian Dandy Volume Two: An Oxford Scholar* – Editor.]

He had taken me to one side at a family party

during the summer for what he called a man-to-man talk and from his opening remarks I gathered that during his youth he had been something of a young gay blade about town. After much clutching at the lapels of his dinner jacket and marching and countermarching across the drawing-room carpet, he confessed how he had conjoined, as he put it, with many attractive young ladies who may not have been thought suitable companions by his parents but whose company he very much enjoyed – especially during the wee, small hours, if I took his meaning!

'Marriage is an excellent and most proper institution, my boy,' Uncle Humphrey had intoned solemnly, 'and I trust that when your time comes to settle down, you have as satisfying and comfortable relationship as has been granted to me with your Aunt Maud. But let us not beat about the bush. Just as it is important for your bride to come to you unsullied, it is of equal import that you too gain experience in ah, "intimate relationships" between the sexes. The best place to do this is preferably far from one's home and in the anonymity of a big city. So if you agree, I propose that you spend the next twelve months in London. You can stay rent free at my old friend Colonel Wright's house in Bedford Square, Bloomsbury, where all your domestic needs will be looked after by Mrs Harrow, the housekeeper. There you will be able to entertain with total discretion any friends of the opposite sex. Furthermore, I will make you an annual allowance to enable you to live at a decent standard of comfort.'

He waved away my effusive words of gratitude.

'No thanks needed, my boy, it's my very real pleasure,' he continued, placing his hand on my shoulder. 'I've already settled fifty thousand pounds on both my daughters and your Aunt will never be able to spend what's left in the bank even if I kick the bucket tomorrow. And in any case, I'd far rather enjoy spending my money now whilst I'm alive than give the damned Government the satisfaction of mopping up thousands of pounds in death duties from my estate.'

It took a while for my parents to be won round to his freewheeling point of view, but in the end they consented, on the strict understanding that I would take up articles with Godfrey, Alan and Colin, the family firm of solicitors, immediately after the year was up.

So I owed a great deal to Uncle Humphrey and though I wrote to the old chap occasionally, I knew how much he thoroughly enjoyed the visits I paid him and Aunt Maud (especially as his two daughters had married and lived far away, cousin Beth in Cornwall and cousin Sarah in the Highlands of Scotland. So I sat down then and there and wrote back, first to my father, telling him that I would return home to Albion Towers two days before the party in York and secondly to Uncle Humphrey, asking him if it would be convenient if I came to see him in Harrogate whilst I was up in Yorkshire for a few days.

When I looked closely at the third and final letter Edwards had given me I saw that it had been posted in France. And yes, the name of the sender, Miss Diana Wigmore, was written on the back of the envelope – what a coincidence! I'll wager she's writing about this party for the King, I thought to myself, and sure enough that is what had made Diana put pen to paper. For the record, diary, I will copy her letter in your pages:

69 Rue General Olivier Norman, Paris

Darling Rupert,

My Mama has just written to me about a grand reception being given in honour of the King on November 15 in York. I gather that your people have also been invited and if you are going to accept then I will go back home as well for a few days. Write, or better still send me a telegram at the above address (trust me to find an apartment in a house numbered soixante-neuf!*) as soon as possible to let me know your plans.*

Have you been keeping well? I suppose your prick has been well-exercised since we last exchanged letters three months ago. You must either write and tell me all about what you have been doing with yourself or tell me all the juicy details if we are to meet back home next month.

Meanwhile, I have been enjoying myself too though I am working hard and not living the Sybaritic life of a lounge lizard like some I could mention! You remember I told you about my affair with Alain. Well, that fizzled out and for more than three weeks I was without a bed-mate for though I had many offers, including several from fellow artists and my landlord Monsieur Cantona, I am choosy as to whose cock I want sheathed in my cunt.

Relief came yesterday with the arrival of a new lodger, an American lad of about our age named Wilson who has come to stay for a month in Paris to perfect his French. He is a handsome young man with a craggy face, a strong nose, well-pronounced cheekbones, a firm mouth and a square jaw. We met on the stairway as I was carrying a kettle of hot water up to my room to make some coffee. I introduced myself to him and I was pleased by the feel of his firm handshake. 'Will you join me for a cup of coffee?' I asked and he thanked me warmly. 'Just let me put some papers in my desk before I forget and I'll be down in three minutes,' he said and I watched with appreciation his muscular, tight backside move quickly up the stairs.

In fact, I was so busy fantasising about Wilson's bum whilst I was preparing the coffee that I spilled some milk all over the front of my blouse. Hell's bells, I said to myself, and without giving it another thought, unbuttoned the garment and threw it in the direction of my laundry basket. There was a muffled cough behind me and there was Wilson, looking rather embarrassed as I turned round and faced him wearing only a thin transparent silk camisole.

'Oh – sorry – I – uh . . .' he stammered.

'No, please don't apologise,' I pleaded, as I watched a slight bulge form in the crotch of his trousers. 'I just spilled some milk over my blouse and had to change it.'

'I can't say I'm sorry,' he said wistfully and it struck me that the yearning expression on his face deserved to be captured on canvas. So I asked Wilson if he would sit for me and to my joy he agreed. 'You'll have to sit quite still for about an hour,' I warned him but he said he would be honoured to be sketched by such a talented artist.

'How do you know I'm talented?' I teased and he replied that the pictures on the wall testified to my

abilities. Well, Wilson proved to be a marvellous model, keeping stock still whilst I worked and when I had finished he came round and looked critically at my drawing. 'I only wish our roles could be reversed and that I could be the artist and you the model,' he commented.

'Why is that?' I asked, slightly puzzled by his remark.

'Because you have such a lovely figure, Diana. I can hardly take my eyes off your beautiful breasts,' he whispered hoarsely, running his hands up the sides of my arms, and I swiftly realised why I had so excited him. Of course, in my haste I had neglected to put on another blouse and all the while Wilson had been gazing intently at my breasts which were only covered by a transparent silk camisole. My titties fairly tingled with anticipation and I felt my nipples pucker with delight as he looked down my body. I took hold of his hands and boldly put them full on my heaving breasts and he sharply exhaled a long drawn out breath as he felt the rigid and upright titties against his palms.

I could see the bulge in his trousers getting bigger which made my pussey moisten and I started to walk backwards, pulling Wilson along with me. It took only three or four steps to reach my bed and we collapsed down upon the sheets as our mouths met in a burning, passionate kiss. His lips were very wet and soft and I could feel his tongue exploring every inch of my mouth whilst his hands roamed across my breasts, squeezing, nipping, and gently caressing the soft white globes, which drove me wild with desire for him. He unzipped my skirt and pulled it down as at the same time I pulled the camisole over my head so that I was now naked except for a pair of frilly white briefs and my stockings which were held up by two red garters.

'Now it's my turn to see more of you,' I said and I

quickly unbuttoned his cream flannels and plunged my hand inside his flies to free his bursting, erect cock as he hastily discarded his shoes and socks. His trousers and drawers soon followed and my eyes fastened upon his thick prick which was standing nicely to attention, a stiff staff up against his flat tummy. I grasped hold of the throbbing tube and ran my fingers down the blue vein which ran down the length of the smooth, warm shaft.

Wilson groaned and put his mouth on my titties, nibbling my nips which rose up like two red bullets. I lifted my bottom to allow him to pull down my knickers and a thrilling wave of pleasure flowed through me as his fingers massaged my hairy pussey and he slid his forefinger inside my oozing cunt whilst I played with his bare cock, slowly rubbing my clenched fingers up and down the hot, pulsing pole.

Our two nude bodies rolled in ecstacy on the bed. His hands were never still, and as he looked lovingly at each part of me, he stroked my breasts, my bottom and my pussey and whispered how gorgeous, how sensual and how desirable I was. 'Then fuck me, please, Wilson,' I murmured, and the dear lad was more than ready to oblige. He climbed on top of me and I spread my legs, eagerly awaiting the arrival of his cock which I still held tightly in my grasp. I guided his knob between my cunney lips and his rock hard prick filled my cunt as we wriggled round until we were both in the most comfortable position for some truly wonderful fucking. I wrapped my feet around his neck as he began to thrust his truncheon in and out of my juicy love channel and I quivered with delight as he began to pump faster and faster, his balls fairly banging against my bum.

'Deeper, Wilson, deeper,' I purred and he pressed his

buttocks together and rammed his tool into me as far as it would go. 'Aaah! Aaah! Keep going, you randy big-cocked boy!' I shrieked, and I shuddered with delight as his prick massaged my clitty and I could feel my cunney sucking at him and I squeezed every time he pulled his cock back for another huge thrust. Now I arched my back, willing the lovely lad on as I pushed my pussey up against him, forcing his cock even deeper inside me and I screamed out my joy as we came together, Wilson shooting a fierce fountain of creamy sperm inside my cunt as my own love juices flowed out of my sated honeypot. We threshed like wild animals, oblivious to everything except the breathtaking currents of the electric force which we had generated between us surging through our bodies.

He rolled off me and lay on his back, his chest heaving up and down as he sought to recover his senses, but his cock, which was glistening with a coating of my pussey juice, was still standing up stiffly and I leaned forward and crammed as much of the silky wet shaft into my mouth as possible. My head bobbed up and down as I greedily gobbled as much of his prick as I could, massaging the sensitive underside with my tongue. I could hear Wilson almost crying with pleasure. Soon I felt his prick go rigid and he spurted jets of sticky semen inside my mouth which I eagerly swallowed until I had milked every last drain of spunk from his trembling tool. His jism had a salty flavour, pleasant enough, but not as tasty as yours, Rupert, so there is no call for you to be jealous!

The grateful boy kissed my lips again and again and thanked me profusely for sucking him off, as, believe it or not, this was the first time he had ever enjoyed the delights of this grand sport. Unbelievably, the poor lad had till now missed out completely on an activity which all men adore. I am sure you will agree that there is not a red-blooded man in the world who can control his excitement once a pair of female lips have fastened themselves upon his knob. But as far as Wilson was concerned, the very idea of girls and boys sucking each other off was alien to him. He had been brought up in a very strict environment and even the mechanics of oral sex were totally unknown to him until he was sixteen when his wise brother-in-law gave him a copy of Dr Nigel Andrews' excellent book Fucking For Beginners. *Unfortunately, he was never given a chance to put into practice what he had learned from Dr Andrews' tome and if we had not been pressed for time I would have shown him how to eat pussey. Hopefully, I will give him his first lesson tomorrow.*

But for now I could only stay for another hour or so as I had to leave for a seminar (you would be amazed at how well I can now converse in French) so we spent the next sixty minutes in fucking until poor Wilson was totally exhausted. Twice more he came inside me and twice I sucked his cock back up to a fine stiffness. We finished this torrid session of love-making by my swallowing the by now understandably diminished quantity of spermy essence from his trembling prick.

Rupert darling, I must close now – but I do hope you will be able to go to York next month. We should have some great fun if old Tum Tum [the lèse-majesté nickname for the corpulent Edward VII – Editor] *is on form.*

All my love,
Diana

I folded the sheets of this *billet doux* back in its envelope and resolved to keep it to copy into the pages of my journal at a later date. So I strode upstairs into my bedroom and locked the letter away in my escritoire. As I did so, I heard a slight noise coming from inside my bathroom. The door was slightly ajar and I peered inside to see that Mary, one of the prettiest maids in the house, was humming a tune whilst she was bending over the bath, polishing the enamel. Although she had her back to me I could tell it was Mary from the colour of her dark, almost black hair and the lissome shape of her body. I passed my tongue over my lips as I surveyed the contours of her ripe backside which, undisguised by a too-tight skirt, stuck out in an extremely provocative fashion.

Like my chum Frank Folkestone is fond of saying, I can resist anything except a pretty bum! I took two paces forward and pinched her glorious bum between my thumb and forefinger. 'Eddie! You randy bugger, stop that at once! Can't you wait till lunch-time?' Mary squealed as she shot up, but she clapped a hand to her mouth in horror when she whirled round and saw that it was the master of the house who had assaulted her. I smiled broadly to put the girl at her ease and said, 'Ah me, lucky Eddie, who I presume is my efficient young footman.'

She gulped with embarrassment and said, 'Yes sir, Eddie Edwards. I'm awfully sorry but I didn't expect you to come up behind me.'

'The fault is all mine and I had no right at all to startle you, but your delicious rounded bottom cheeks were simply too arousing as you bent over the bath. Please forgive me, Mary, it won't happen again,' I added, with as much sincerity as

I could muster, which was not a great deal, especially when even as I spoke, my cock began to swell up alarmingly, forming a noticeable bulge between my legs.

'Oh, that's quite all right, sir, I'm not cross with you – it was just being caught unawares which made me jump,' she said, turning back to finish her work.

I considered her cute arse again and placed a hand on each soft, rounded buttock. 'Oooh, you'd better not do that, sir. You really mustn't. Someone might come in.'

Amused and aroused now by this form of surrender I unbuttoned her skirt and pulled it to the floor. Then I tugged down her crisp white knickers and she stepped out of them before resuming her labours. I smoothed my hands along the creamy cool skin of her appetising bum cheeks and then slid my right hand between her legs. She neatly trapped it by squeezing her thighs together, leaving me to wrestle with my fly buttons with my left hand whilst I tickled the entrance to her honeypot with my imprisoned fingers.

My trousers and drawers now joined Mary's clothes on the floor and I begged her to release my hand so I could replace it with something more pleasing. She moved her head round and with shining eyes looked down at my hard, erect member. 'You'll have to go in by the tradesmen's entrance, sir, I can't risk letting you have my cunney till next week,' she said, and wriggled back so that her head and upper body were bent quite low over the bath as she pushed her glorious backside upwards and opened her legs to give me fair view of the tiny, puckered brown rosette. I knelt down and picked up a sponge and soaped my pulsating boner before parting her buttocks with my hands and pushing my uncapped helmet into the cleft between them.

'Yes, do go, sir. Go carefully though as you stick that nice thick length of cock up my bum,' she said excitedly.

I angled her legs a little further apart to afford an even better view of her winking little rear dimple and gently eased my knob forward. For a few seconds I encountered resistance but then her sphincter muscle relaxed and I slid my rigid rod in and out of her tight arse-hole, plunging in and out of the now widened rim as Mary reached back and spread her cheeks even further, jerking her bum in time to my rhythm as I wrapped one arm around her breasts, squeezing each of them in turn and snaking my other arm round her waist to frig her wet pussey as she whimpered with pleasure, squirming and wriggling about to such an extent that I had to work hard to keep my cock inside her.

Mary's bottom continued to respond gaily to every pistoning thrust as again and again I drove home, my balls bouncing against her soft buttocks. Then I shoved my shaft in to the hilt, corking her to the very limit. I stayed still for a moment and then jerked my hips slowly as I felt the first sweet stirrings of an approaching spend and with a strangled cry I shot a copious emission of gushing jism inside her bottom. As I spurted into her bum-hole, I continued to work my prick back and forth until, with an audible 'plop', I withdrew my shrinking organ from Mary's well-lathered nether orifice.

'Ooh, that was nice, sir. Could you suck my cunney now?' she asked.

Well, much as we would have both enjoyed a continuation of this frolic, *tempus fugit* – Mary had to finish her household chores and I had to compose myself for my luncheon with Nancy Carrington. I noticed a large blob of spunk had dripped down from Mary's bottom on to the marble floor which she wiped clean with a cloth.

'Just as well we didn't have that lovely bottom-fuck in the bedroom,' I commented as I hauled up my trousers. 'I wouldn't want to damage any of Colonel Wright's rare Persian carpets.'

This remark made Mary giggle and she said, 'Oh, spunk marks are no problem, sir. Whenever the Colonel has one of his special parties, we always manage to clean up without any trouble.'

'Special parties?' I queried and Mary put her finger to my lips. 'Please don't tell anyone I mentioned anything to you, sir. I thought you knew about the monthly reunions or I wouldn't have said a word about them.'

'Don't worry, my lips are sealed,' I said, intrigued by her concern. 'But I haven't had the pleasure of meeting the Colonel himself. He just happens to be a close friend of my Uncle Humphrey and agreed to rent the house to him whilst he is in India. I seem to recall my Uncle telling me that the Colonel was invited to join some government inquiry and will spend twelve months out East.'

Mary nodded and confirmed my vague memory

of the conversation with Uncle Humphrey. 'Colonel Wright's the deputy chairman of the Royal Commission on Native Education. The Prime Minister himself asked him to serve and so he felt he could not refuse. "I don't really want to go, Mary," he said to me before he left, "but the other day Mr Lloyd-George all but promised me a knighthood if I accept the job."

' "Never mind, sir," I said, as I squeezed his balls. "I'll bring my friend Sally round and we'll have that nice whoresome threesome you've always dreamed about." '

Was I dreaming or did this pretty young maid actually promise her former employer that she and another girl would share his bed? I looked at her in astonishment and burst out, 'You said *what*?'

She repeated her remark and I said incredulously, 'You were squeezing the Colonel's balls? That was rather forward behaviour, was it not?'

'Not really,' she replied, shrugging her shoulders. 'After all, he had his cock in my cunney at the time.'

I stared at her in amazement as she added, 'Don't look so surprised, sir. Cuthbert might be fifty-eight in February but I can tell you it's quite true that there's many a good tune played on an old fiddle. He takes longer to come than younger men but that's all to the good because so many boys of my age come too quickly.'

'Did he fuck you very often?' I wondered, and this question brought a satisfied smile to her lips.

'As often as I wanted,' she rejoined pertly. 'If I say so myself, I'm not short of a cock when I want one.'

'I'm sure you're not, Mary, you're a very attractive young lady. Frankly, I'm just rather curious as to how you two became involved.'

'Oh, that's easily explained,' she said lightly, picking up her box of cloths and polishes. 'I'll tell you how if you don't mind following me into the bedroom across the hall. I know it's not being used right now but Mr Bristow asked me to give it the once over every week in case we have a sudden guest coming to stay.'

Mr Bristow, I should mention here, was the butler I had inherited from Colonel Wright. Sadly, his aged father had died suddenly a few days previous to this conversation and naturally I had agreed at once to his request for a week's compassionate leave of absence. In the meantime, the estimable cook-housekeeper, Mrs Harrow, was taking charge of all matters below stairs.

'Certainly, I'll come along – you'll now have a witness if Mr Bristow alleges that you failed to carry out his instructions,' I joked as I followed Mary into the second bedroom. I sat on the bed whilst she told me of how she first became aware of Colonel Wright's attentions.

She told me, 'It all began about eighteen months ago just after I had joined the household. Although I was only seventeen, I had already sampled two or three cocks in my pussey before I came here. However, I hadn't been fucked for a good few weeks until a few days before this incident when I had let PC Shackleton thread me up against the back garden wall.

'Well, I went to bed well satisfied and, though I slept like a top, for once I woke before Mrs

Harrow knocked on my door and I remember snaking my arms above my head for a long stretch, thinking back with a smile about the little knee-trembler I had enjoyed with my randy copper, before kicking off the bedclothes and springing to my feet.

'Now I never wear anything in bed so I was stark naked as I padded over to the window, threw back the curtains and opened the window. As I gazed delightedly at the bright dawn sunshine my hand strayed down to my little nookie. I was twisting my curly pussey hair around my fingers and gently stroking myself around my crack when I heard what sounded like a sharp intake of breath from underneath my window. Was it a stray cat perhaps or was there some dirty beast down there spying on me?

'There was an easy way to find out – I withdrew for a moment and returned with my chamber pot which I had used during the night but I added the contents of my water jug to fill the pot almost to the brim. Then I raised the window sash to the highest level and leaned out, feeling the cool morning air tease my rosy nipples into little erect buds. I distinctly heard a low, furtive moan coming from down below which confirmed that it was indeed a Peeping Tom hiding in the dense foliage. So I withdrew for a moment and came back again, leaning out to tip the contents of the chamber pot out the window!

'An anguished yell told me that I had scored a direct hit on whoever had been spying on me – but to my horror, who should emerge wet headed, spluttering with rage, with his trousers round his knees and his hand round his bare cock but the Master himself!'

'The dirty old so-and-so! It served him right to be drenched in your you-know-what!' I exclaimed.

'Ah! But you've jumped to conclusions, sir, though of course I did the very same thing as well,' Mary remonstrated, touching my lips with her finger. 'The truth of the matter was that the Colonel, who has always suffered from insomnia, had woken with the dawn and had decided to potter around the garden. It was by pure coincidence that he happened to be outside my window when suddenly he had been caught short and rather than trudge back inside the house, he decided to relieve his bladder in the garden. He had just finished his piddle when he heard me open the window. He looked up and, well, I could hardly blame him for becoming speechless with astonished delight when he saw my naked body above him.'

Mary paused for breath and then continued with a grin, 'Well, poor old Cuthbert could hardly shout up anything to me or the other servants might have looked out to see what was going on. So he rushed inside, changed his clothes and came straight up to see me. I had already half a mind to start packing my bags but as soon as Cuthbert came into my room he began apologising for his rudeness and explained the circumstances which had inadvertently led him to the sorry situation in which he now found himself.

'And as for giving me the sack, nothing could be further from his thoughts. Instead, he insisted on presenting me with a gold sovereign to compensate, as he put it, for any distress I might have felt about the wretched incident which he hoped could now be forgotten.

'I thought this was more than generous and so I asked him to sit on the bed. "You deserve a proper view of what you only caught a glimpse of earlier," I said and tossing back my shimmering curls and running my tongue lewdly over my pouting lips, I unknotted the cord of the bathrobe I had hastily donned along with a pair of white cotton knickers when I realised that the Cuthbert was coming upstairs. I slid out of the robe, arching my spine and sucking in my breath to give Cuthbert a wonderful full frontal view of my big, luscious breasts. You haven't seen them yet, have you, sir? Well, take my word, I'm lucky enough to have two beauties and I don't mind admitting that I'm very proud of them.

'Anyway, I took my raspberry nipples between my fingers and tweaked them up till they blushed a deep red and grew stiffly erect. "By Gad!" said Cuthbert as I began to knead my firm, uptilted titties and then, planting my hands on my hips, shook my breasts at him energetically, trying hard not to giggle as I saw a huge swelling start to form in Cuthbert's lap.

'Then ever so slowly I began to pull down my knickers, wriggling round so that by the time I'd pulled them down I was facing the wall and he could see my bare bottom. "Oh my God, this is too much!" he cried out, and when I turned round, with my hand over my pussey, there was Cuthbert with his trousers ripped open, pulling out his thick, throbbing truncheon, the uncapped ruby dome bobbing gaily, as, panting with desire, he frenziedly frigged himself at a great pace.

'I thought that he would prefer me not to gawp at him whilst he brought himself off so I turned back and waggled my bum at him again. Then I gazed at him briefly over my shoulder and flashed him a smile as I parted my legs and bent forward with my arms dangling forward until my hands were almost touching the carpet. This way poor Cuthbert had an even more tantalising view of my firm, gleaming bum cheeks and the dark, secret cleft between them which even as he watched began to moisten with my tangy cunney juice.

'A strangled cry was enough to tell me that Cuthbert was shooting his load and sure enough I straightened up and looked back to see a tiny fountain of creamy white froth shoot out of the top of his twitching tool.

'I dropped to my knees to lap up his manly essence, as I adore the salty taste of hot, fresh jism but as I dived down a second burst of sperm jetted out of his cock straight into my right eye! "I would have preferred to have sucked you off," I said to Cuthbert, and he looked sadly down at his shrivelling shaft and said that he would be very grateful if I would meet him in the library any time after noon as these days he wouldn't be able to raise another stand till around lunch-time.'

This mention of luncheon reminded me that I had an appointment for which I was in grave danger of being late. I looked at my watch and asked Mary if we could continue this fascinating discussion in the library at around five o'clock. 'Oh yes, I'd love to, sir,' she replied promptly, picking up her box of cleaning materials. She then shot me a wicked little smile and added, 'That's on the understanding, of course, that we can have a nice snogging session as well.'

I replied that this was a condition I was more than happy to accept. Then, after a quick wash and brush up, I went downstairs and Edwards confirmed that Harrods had delivered the flowers. After helping me on with my hat and coat he gave me the large, colourful bouquet of chrysanthemums before opening the front door. 'I expect to return home around three o'clock,' I informed him, and set off to walk round to Nancy Carrington's house. Thankfully, the rain had stopped, though it was still quite cold and I was glad that I had worn one of Mr Rabinowitz's warm overcoats even for the short three minute journey to the far corner of Bedford Square.

Nancy Carrington's Negro butler must have seen me climb the short flight of steps for he opened the door before I had a chance to ring the bell. 'Good-afternoon, sir. It's Mr Mountjoy, isn't it?' he said in a deep American-accented drawl. 'May I take your hat and coat? Miss Carrington is receiving her guests in the drawing-room.'

I looked up at the tall, wide-shouldered man. He was a very handsome fellow of a light chocolate hue and, although his frizzy curly hair was jet black, his finely chiselled features suggested that he must have had at least one European grandparent. Presumably he is an old family retainer of Nancy's family, I thought to myself, as he opened the drawing-room door and announced my arrival to his mistress.

'Rupert, how super to see you – and what lovely flowers you've brought, you kind boy,' cried Nancy Carrington, who rose up from the sofa on which she had been sitting next to another extremely attractive, slightly older woman. 'I'm so pleased that you were able to join me for lunch today as I wanted you to meet a dear friend who I met in Paris earlier this year. Rupert, it is my great pleasure to introduce you to Countess Marussia of Samarkand. Marussia, this is my nice new neighbour Mr Rupert Mountjoy.

'Now I will have to ask the two of you to excuse me for a few moments as I have some last minute instructions for the kitchen staff.'

As Nancy bustled out of the room I walked over and, taking the Countess's hand in my own, raised her fingers to my lips. '*Enchanté, Comtesse,*' I murmured. By George, she was a stunning lady, nearer thirty than twenty perhaps, with long reddish hair, a pale face, and big brown eyes. She was beautifully formed with high breasts, a lithe, slender body and then and there I would have wagered a thousand pounds that her long legs, hidden under her skirt, were as stylish as I expected.

'I am delighted to make your acquaintance, Mr Mountjoy,' said this delicious creature in a sensual low voice. 'Nancy tells me that you have recently graduated from Oxford University. Did you ever come across my cousin Celestine Dushanbe there by any chance?'

Had I ever come across Celestine Dushanbe? How I wish I could have replied in the affirmative for Celestine was without doubt one of the prettiest, most desirable girls in the whole of Oxford and the surrounding county. Like many others, I had unsuccessfully sought her favours but these were only bestowed upon the Honourable Michael Bailey, the handsome captain of the University fencing team and (it was rumoured) the young Lord Arkleigh who travelled up to dine with her almost every weekend from his Hertfordshire estate.

'Alas, no,' I replied with a sad little smile. 'I know of her, of course, but she was always surrounded by a bevy of admirers.'

'I'm sure she was,' said Countess Marussia, returning my smile. 'Celestine threw herself into her work with great passion and like all dedicated students, she practised what she preached, though of course in Celestine's case she thoroughly enjoyed the experience.'

'Did she, Countess? Why, what was she studying?' I asked politely, but nearly fell over backwards when the Countess answered, 'Human sexuality. Dear Celestine was one of a small group of researchers working with Dr Trevor Tyler, the internationally noted specialist on masturbation, on his new book *The Facts Of Life*, a much needed book which will be published early next year by Messrs Dyott & Gradegate.'

'I must remember to order a copy from Hatchards,' I said, recovering my composure and adding (for I had decided that the Countess was obviously a fellow free spirit), 'although I would have thought that *Fucking For Beginners* by Nigel Andrews might have already covered this ground.'

'Not really,' said the Countess, shaking her head, 'because excellent as Dr Andrews' volume is for, say, newly married couples, it can only be bought *sub rosa* by enlightened people who have already shaken off the atmosphere of guilt, fear and ignorance about sex and subscribe to such journals as *The Oyster* or *The Jenny Everleigh Diaries*.

'Dr Tyler, on the other hand, is composing a manual for the complete relationship between the sexes, starting from the premise that though love-making is one of the few subjects in which we all have an interest, the understanding of many people of their bodies is frequently minimal. There is still a large body of opinion which treats sexual desire as a dangerous animal that has to be kept muzzled. At present, the few sex education books available prescribe abstinence and chastity – such hypocrisy when one considers the bedroom sport enjoyed by Society at country house parties and the *laissez-faire* attitude taken by your very own King Edward!'

As I nodded my agreement, I gnawed at my lower lip as I recalled the one opportunity I had missed of getting closer to Celestine Dushanbe. I had noticed a small advertisement in the University weekly newspaper for volunteers to take part in scientific research. I had expressed a vague interest to a friend but had hastily abandoned the thought of replying to the box number when he had opined that in all probability the advertiser was looking out for people to test their new medical pills and potions. I confessed this foolish blunder to the Countess who laughed and said, 'I must tell you that I remember Celestine writing to me about why she had placed that particular advertisement. She was discussing the "doggie position" with Dr Tyler who had told her that some people frowned upon it as being too animalistic although anatomically it is a most natural position of sexual congress.

'But look, you can read Celestine's report for yourself. One of the reasons I am here is that both Nancy and I have been asked by Dr Tyler to make any suggestions about his manuscript as we are both self-proclaimed liberated ladies. We were reading the section of his book which deals with Celestine's appreciation of being taken from behind.'

She got up and walked across to a paper strewn table, picked up a sheet and passed it to me, saying, 'Come and sit down and glance through this page. I would be most interested any comment you might have to make.'

I obeyed and read the following from an essay on sexual positions by Dr Tyler: '*My colleague Miss C.D. tried out rear entry with her boy friend and writes, in her own uncensored words: "I placed myself on my hands and knees, bending forward and throwing up my bottom cheeks as high as possible. My lover inserted his penis and began working it in and out of my love channel. He pressed heavily against me but there was no problem in supporting his weight. Perhaps this was because I was on my hands and knees with my back and thigh muscles (the strongest in the body) working.*

"The experience was thoroughly enjoyable as both his hands were free to fondle my breasts, legs and buttocks and he could bring his fingers round to my front and play with my clitoris which afforded an additional pleasure."

'How very interesting,' I observed as I passed the sheet back to the Countess. '"Doggie fashion" happens to be one of my personal favourites although I am sure there are many sexual positions about which I am completely ignorant.'

'Oh, come now,' she said roguishly. 'I am sure that a good-looking young fellow like you has experimented widely in this field. Mind, the Indian *Kama Sutra* lists more than twenty major positions for fucking though Trevor Tyler insists that in practice there are really only six and all the others are simply variants.'

She patted my thigh and was about to say more when Nancy flounced back into the room carrying my chrysanthemums in a crystal bowl. 'There, don't flowers brighten up the room?' she said brightly. 'Now I hope you two are getting on famously.'

'Indeed we are,' I replied, struggling up from the deep cushions of the sofa. 'The Countess has just been telling me about the proofs you are checking of Dr Trevor Tyler's wonderfully interesting new book.'

'Ah yes, I'm so pleased you approve, Rupert. So many people have hidebound attitudes to an activity without which, let's face it, the human race would cease to exist! Anyhow, luncheon is served so you will have to escort both Marussia and myself into the dining-room.'

'That will be my pleasure,' I said with a bow. So I walked into the dining-room with a lovely girl on each arm. The marvellous meal we ate testified to the wisdom of household cooks attending a course at Mrs Bickler's Academy of Domestic Science. We dined sumptuously on *Terrine d'aubergines et poivres rouges aux saveurs de Provence* followed by a tasty *filet de flétan roti sur aromates au fumet de fin rouge* and as the main course succulent *côtelettes d'agneau roties à la chapelure provençale et legumes d'été* finished off with *assiette de fruits du moment au Sabayon de Kirsch et sorbet cassis*. [Aubergines, halibut in a red wine sauce, lamb cutlets, and a fresh fruit salad! – Editor]

We were attentively served by Hutchinson, the Negro butler, Standlake, and two housemaids and we drank at least two bottles of a very smooth Chablis as Hutchinson was always on hand to ensure that our glasses were never empty. Then we returned to the drawing-room for *petit fours* and (in honour of Marussia) *thé Russe avec citron*.

By this time we were all slightly flushed and feeling very well disposed to each other. Indeed, Nancy's shiny blonde hair, which she had been wearing in rather severe brushed curls, now hung in long, silky strands down to her shoulders. With Nancy in the middle we were all sitting on the luxuriously soft sofa when, after serving us glasses of hot lemon tea, Hutchinson left the room and closed the door behind him. Nancy squeezed both my hand and Marussia's and said, 'My dears, you must try some of the special thirty-year-old cognac I was given by Monsieur Istvan Tihanyi in Paris.'

'Not Monsieur Istvan Tihanyi who owns the dildo manufactory near Drancy?' said Marussia excitedly.

'Yes, the very same. Why, do you know him, Marussia?'

'Of course I do – Istvan has been a close friend for several years. Only last summer he fucked me beautifully after Senator Lipmann's Quatorze Juillet ball in Paris.

Nancy heaved herself up and walked to the sideboard and brought out the bottle and a silver tray with three balloon shaped brandy glasses placed upon it. She poured out generous measures of vintage cognac and Marussia suggested we drank a toast. 'To our charming hostess,' I suggested. Nancy thanked me and added, 'Coupled with the names of my two dear friends Marussia and Rupert.' We then drank a toast to Marussia's hero, Tamburlaine the Great, who in the fourteenth century had made Samarkand the chief economic and cultural centre of mid Asia. Then followed toasts to the United States of America, King Edward VII, Prince Adrian of the Netherlands (who often escorted the Countess on the Continent) and then to Monsieur Istvan Tihanyi's penis which the girls assured me was of heroic proportions.

'Nancy, how did you come to meet Istvan?' demanded Marussia. 'Did you meet him at his place of work?'

'Not at first,' answered Nancy. 'Our first meeting was at the Moulin Rouge where we were both guests at a party given by the American community in Paris to celebrate the fiftieth birthday of His Excellency, Mr Barry Gray, our new Ambassador to France. Istvan and I began talking and I must say I was fascinated when he informed me of his business.'

At this point I interrupted the conversation and said, 'Forgive me ladies, but I must confess ignorance of this gentleman and his work. Perhaps one of you could enlighten me.'

'Certainly, Rupert,' said Nancy cheerfully. 'Istvan Tihanyi owns an exclusive dildo factory patronised by the *crème de la crème* of European Society. His speciality is the production of ladies' comforters, individually made for clients based on the dimensions of the husband or lover as required.'

'How fascinating,' I commented, 'but I am rather surprised there is any demand for such artefacts. Surely there is a sufficiency of living male members to satisfy any need?'

Countess Marussia answered my question. 'Alas, no, for there are many women of the very highest standing in Society who are in great need of a good godemiches. To begin with, think of all the married women who cannot count on being regularly fucked by their husbands. For example, those married to men of business who have to be away from home, often for days on end. Then there are service wives who are often separated from their menfolk for months, and sometimes when these men return they are so fatigued from fighting that they are unable to resume their marital duties for a considerable while. Finally, one must never forget those unfortunate ladies whose husbands are no longer capable of performing their conjugals for other reasons such as over-indulgence in imbibing, and those, such as dear Lady Bertha Bumble, who have been tragically widowed at an early age, though in her case of course, she has been consoled more than adequately by her brother-in-law, Lord Radlett, who fucks her every other Thursday afternoon whilst his wife plays bridge at the local Constitutional Club.'

My hostess nodded her agreement and added, 'So you see, dear Rupert, there is a genuine and continuous demand for a discreet but effective substitute for a stiff, hard cock. Anyhow, many ladies commission a dildo of the same dimensions as a particularly well-loved prick and gentlemen being forced for one reason or another to leave their lovers, also contact him to produce a matching set of basin, ewer, soap dish and dildo for the boudoir.'

She stood up and went back to the sideboard from which she brought out a small silver box which she placed in my hands as she sat down again and said, 'After spending three nights of lusty abandon with Monsieur Tihanyi, I was thrilled to receive from him this charming momento of a glorious fuck.'

I opened the box and looked down upon a superbly fashioned ceramic cock nestling on a small, plump velvet cushion. It was painted in pale blue and further decorated in a complicated yet somehow familiar design of maroon and gold diamonds and hoops. Nancy must have read my mind for she commented, 'You may recognise the pattern, Rupert, for these are Monsieur

Tihanyi's racing colours.'

This remark jogged my memory and I now recalled wildly cheering on the jockey who was wearing these selfsame colours as he won the Portnoy Stakes on a game little filly called Lady Norma at Goodwood the previous summer. It had truly been a glorious Goodwood as far as I was concerned for although the weather had not been as fine as usual, I had placed ten pounds each way on Lady Norma at odds of seven to one and later in the afternoon I accepted the invitation to mount Mrs Chelmsford in a private tent whilst everyone else was watching the last race.

'It is certainly a very beautiful gift,' I murmured softly, as I handed the box back to Nancy. 'And if, as you say, this dildo is modelled on his prick, Monsieur Tihanyi is certainly an extremely well-endowed gentleman though I am sure that even a superb dildo cannot match the feel of the genuine article.'

She smiled sweetly and said with a naughty gleam in her eyes, 'Oh, Rupert, I think you would be surprised how many ladies actually prefer the substitute to even the thickest, real live cock. After all, a dildo doesn't shoot off and go limp too quickly and one can finely tune the speed and force of entry to one's personal taste. Perhaps you would like to see for yourself how easily it can be used? I am sure Marussia would have no objection in helping me with a little demonstration.'

'It would be my pleasure,' said the Countess, rising from the sofa. 'Come, let us adjourn to the bedroom.'

I followed the two women into Nancy's bedroom where I was invited to sit on a chair whilst they undressed. After kicking off their shoes they unbuttoned each other's blouses, and then, sitting on the bed, they unhinged their suspenders and peeled off their stockings, giggling merrily away as they saw my excited penis swell up to form a mountainous bulge in my lap.

Now they embraced each other and whilst kissing passionately on the lips they pulled off their camisoles and lay back, entwined in each other's arms, wearing nothing but flimsy silk knickers which appeared to be of identical design. Marussia noticed this as well and remarked, 'Ah, I see that you also patronise Madame Vazelina of Berwick Street, Soho for your underwear.'

'Yes, I am a regular patron,' replied Nancy, stroking her magnificently large creamy breasts which were tipped with delightfully rounded areolas and exquisitely fashioned nipples which were already pointing out so juicily that I longed to throw myself upon her and suck these gorgeous little red strawberries.

But Countess Marussia's hands were now upon them and Nancy placed her palms on the other girl's bare breasts which, though not of her size, also jutted out proudly and were capped by equally large tawney stalks which were brought up to full erection by Nancy tweaking them between her long fingers.

'Help us off with our knickers, Rupert, there's a dear lad,' said Nancy, and the girls raised their bottoms invitingly as I walked over rather awkwardly, trying to shield my raging hard-on as I pulled down their remaining garments, though the sight of their nude pussies almost made me 'cream my jeans', as my Yankee pal Paul Mallock would have put it, then and there. I would have given anything to have sunk my throbbing tool into either Nancy's notch, which was delicately covered by a curtain of frizzy golden hair, or Marussia's pussey, which was more thickly masked by a thatch of reddish curls, but for the moment it was obvious that the presence of my cock would have been considered *de trop*, so I sat on the edge of the bed and relaxed as I watched the girls enjoy themselves together.

Marussia's left hand continued to toy with Nancy's breast whilst her right hand slid down the American girl's snow white belly and into the mound of golden pussey hair through which I could now see the pouting lips of her cunney. I leaned forward to see Marussia's forefinger disappear between these lips and the girls exchanged a further series of voluptuous kisses until Marussia broke off the embrace to nuzzle her lips against one of Nancy's nipples, drawing it deep inside her eager mouth. Nancy gasped as Marussia, who was now firmly taking control of this tribadistic encounter, now had two of her fingers sliding in and out of Nancy's cunt, moving them so swiftly that they were almost vibrating. Her thumb skated rapidly back and forth over the protruding clitty and Nancy arched her back, squirming with delight as she jerked herself into a splendid little orgasm.

Now it was Nancy's turn to repay her pretty

bed-mate who turned her back on her, sliding her delicious bum cheeks on Nancy's dripping pussey. Nancy pushed her hips forward and the two rocked in rhythm as she caressed Marussia's breasts from behind, flicking up the large, tawny stalks to peak erection. Then she dipped a hand down to the Countess's bushy *mons veneris*, itself a shapely hillock of firm flesh, surmounted with its rich profusion of reddish curls. Her finger and thumb soon found the hardening clitty which popped out between Marussia's cunney lips and made her gasp, 'A-a-h-r-r-e! A-a-h-r-r-e! You clever girl, now please finish me off with your tongue and Monsieur Tihanyi's dildo, there's a dear.'

Nancy slid out from under her and as she knelt between the other girl's long legs, she said, 'Mmmm, I can smell your juicy cunt from here, Marussia.' She lowered her head between her legs and began kissing her full, gorgeous pussey. I craned my head forward to see Nancy run her tongue along the full length of Marussia's parted cunney lips, stopping at the hardened little ball of her clitty which she gave her best attention, nibbling from side to side, up and down, as the Countess threw back her head and writhed with passion.

'Yes, yes! You're so good, Nancy. Keep sucking! Eat my pussey! Oh, how I adore it!' she cried, as Nancy's right hand snaked out, searching for the dildo. I aided her by opening the box and placing the instrument in her hand and gazed with increasing interest as Nancy now nudged the tip of dildo between the yielding lips of Marussia's cunt. Then she began fucking her in earnest with the superbly-fashioned dildo, sliding the thick china shaft in and out of her dripping honeypot. 'Further! Harder! Faster!' yelled out the Countess, as, with a final wrenching shudder, she gained her release, yelping with happiness as waves of ecstasy coursed through her body.

They were both still so fired up from this fray that they squealed their approval as I began to tear off my clothes. As soon as I was stark naked I threw myself upon the bed, rolled the two squealing girls over on their sides so that their gorgeous bare bottoms were open to view.

But how was I to solve the ticklish situation of which girl to fuck first? As the snooker player said when presented with a choice of colours, I had to decide whether I should go for the pink or the brown! What a dilemma! I had no wish to cause offence so I was extremely relieved when Nancy called out, 'Marussia, as it was my idea to ask Rupert round this afternoon, I think this gives me the right to claim the first fuck.'

Well, that solved the problem well enough so I took my meaty cock in my hand and pushed my stiff shaft in the smooth valley between the rounded cheeks of Nancy's arse and attempted to force a passage between them.

'Aaah! What a thick prick! But please don't go up my bum, Rupert, I would really prefer that hard hot cock in my cunney!' panted my kind hostess.

I needed no further urging as Nancy lifted her bottom slightly to effect an easy lodgement for my pulsating prick which slid into her moist crack from behind with the utmost ease. I embedded my shaft almost up to the root until my belly was squeezed against her bum and lay still for a moment. At this juncture Marussia entered the fray and nestled her head on Nancy's bosom and began licking and lapping at her lovely erect titties whilst she frigged Nancy's clitty with one hand and her own clitty with the other. I now started to pump my trusty tool in and out of Nancy's squelchy love channel as Marussia continued to frig her from the front. It was all so exciting that I was spent far quicker than I would have liked, though I squirted so many jets of frothy white cream into Nancy's cunt that I could swear that I felt my balls lighten as the delicious thrills of my climax tingled throughout every inch of my perspiring body.

I lay back, heaving with exhaustion, as Marussia now lifted her head from Nancy's titties and said to her, 'Well, darling, as you've now had the first fuck, I'm surely entitled to the first taste of Rupert's succulent chopper.'

'Of course you are, my love,' said Nancy generously, and in a trice, Marussia's hands were clamped around my semi-stiff shaft. 'But do allow me to assist you.'

Nancy sat up and perched on my chest. I felt Marussia's lips envelop the tip of my cock as she began licking all round the edge of my knob. As she started to suck noisily on my now iron-hard stiffstander, Nancy moved up to place her pussey over my mouth so I could tongue her cunney. I sighed with delight as Marussia's wicked tongue now began to lap around the sensitive underside of my shaft, making it ache with unslaked lust. Now she sucked in my helmet, teasing my knob against the roof of her mouth with her tongue and in no time at all I felt the surge of a powerful spend making its way up from my ballsack.

Marussia sensed this and withdrew her skilful tongue for a moment or two before returning to the attack as I continued to slide my tongue through the damp, blonde pussey hairs of Nancy's cunt, letting the tip of my tongue burrow between her pouting pink cunney lips. But when Marussia squeezed her hand round the base of my cock, sucking me harder and harder, I simply could no longer contain myself. My lusty love truncheon pulsed in her mouth as I let out a small cry and jetted spurt after spurt of creamy spunk inside her mouth. She gulped down every drop of my masculine essence and murmured with satisfaction as she licked the last drains from round the head of my gleaming prick which was only slowly losing its stiffness.

All the while I was trying to stimulate Nancy into a spend by nibbling on her clitty and sliding my fingers in and out of her sopping slit. Alas, it was to no avail and the charming girl said regretfully, 'I don't think I can get there without a cock in my cunt.'

Marussia immediately offered to frig her with Monsieur Tihanyi's dildo but then I offered my own organ because, if she could wait ten minutes or so for me to regain my strength, I would be delighted to fuck her again.

'Could you really do it again so soon, Rupert? My, you must have a superb constitution,' Nancy said excitedly with her bright blue eyes shining with lewd anticipation of a second sheathing of my stalk in her cunney.

I swallowed hard and said with a small smile, 'Well, I can usually rise to the occasion three times without having to retire from the game. At school, when we used to play Mother Thumb and her Four Daughters in the dormitory, I could usually manage four spends with only a short break between them though Harry Barr, who is now the Rural Dean of Coketown, could sometimes come five or even six times virtually without stopping at all.'

'I would like to meet this gentleman,' said Marussia instantly, but I shook my head and said, 'No, I don't believe you would, Countess. Most unfortunately, poor Harry became a confirmed homosexualist whilst studying for the priesthood and I shudder to think where he puts his prick these days.'

'What a waste,' sighed Marussia, as she took hold of my dangling shaft and idly began to rub it up and down in her clenched fist. To Nancy's and my great joy, Marussia's frigging was all my shaft needed to begin swelling up to its former glorious state and when it was standing as proudly high as before, Marussia relinquished her grip in favour of Nancy, who clutched my cock in her hand as she pulled my face towards hers and sank her naughty little tongue in my mouth. I stroked her damp blonde bush of pussey hair as she lay back and relaxed, her head supported by her hands whilst I clambered upon her without delay. Immediately she parted her legs to allow me to kneel in front of her open cunney and then Nancy took my rampant rod and guided it directly inside her wet, welcoming cunt.

Although I was admittedly tired from our previous exploits, I think this was the best fuck of all. How exquisitely her velvet cunney walls clung to my cock as she sinuously moved her hips whilst I pistoned my prick up and down, my balls smacking lewdly against her backside with every forward thrust. I pounded in and out of her pussey, my hands gripping her firm, fleshy bum cheeks as we bounced up and down on the soft mattress.

'Oh Rupert, you lovely big-cocked boy! Fuck my juicy cunt with your thick prick!' she gasped, as I thrust home, sliding my shaft home in and out of her marvellous muff. Several times I thought I would spend before her but somehow I managed to hold back till she was ready for me. Again and again, faster and faster, I fucked the sweet girl until with a hoarse wail she achieved a tremendous climax, writhing uncontrollably as a multiple series of spends racked their way through her.

As Nancy had orgasmed I pulled out my twitching tool and reared over her. I gripped my cock and gave it two or three convulsive jerks until a huge fountain of salty sperm spouted out, arcing out towards her breasts, splashing her nipples, streaming down towards her belly button and into her soaking golden thatch.

'Oh how wonderful!' breathed Marussia, who had naturally been watching avidly, frigging herself unashamedly as she saw me rub the spunk around Nancy's erect nipples and all over her tummy. I moved over and squatted over Marussia with my bottom against her face as I leaned down and caressed her palpitating pussey with my tongue, licking up her tangy love juice, as she lifted her head and took my ballsack into her mouth, nibbling my balls through the hairy, wrinkled skin whilst I continued to stimulate her cunt, flicking my tongue in and out of her juicy love channel.

Now Nancy slid her head between my thigh and Marussia's body and began to gobble greedily on my glistening shaft which had miraculously still retained its stiffness (perhaps because I had not shot my total sticky load over Nancy's nipples). She moved round so that she could take my cock in her mouth and she sucked hard upon it, moving her lips from tip to balls and back again, faster and faster, intoxicated like Marussia and myself by the sheer ecstasy of this grand, uninhibited three-way fuck. My prick pulsed against the back of her throat, releasing a further frothy flood of hot jism and she greedily swallowed all my creamy emission as Marussia also spent, filling my mouth with her aromatic love juices, which I also gulped down, as together the three of us ran the course to a complete and totally satisfying fulfilment.

We lay quietly for a few minutes and Marussia asked Nancy and myself if we had planned to go up to Scotland for the rest of the season. 'My companion Prince Adrian of the Netherlands has taken over a house in the Highlands,' she told us, 'and you'd both be very welcome to join us.

You'd be sure to flush out many a gamecock from its covert, Nancy, whilst you, Rupert, would certainly enjoy our rather eccentric version of the Highland Fling let alone the complex routines of our all-nude eightsome reel.'

'I'm sure I would love it,' I said politely, 'but alas, my engagement book is full until the New Year.'

She was about to reply when suddenly Marussia's body stiffened and she said in an urgent, worried voice, 'Hold on a moment, I am sure I heard someone coming.'

'It could be any one of us,' I said wittily.

'No, I mean I thought I heard someone enter the room,' she continued, with a startled look on her face.

Nancy looked across at her and kissed her engorged nipple. 'Don't worry, that will only be Standlake the butler. Whenever I take any guests into the bedroom, he usually comes in after an appropriate length of time to see whether his services are required – either for myself or any other girl who might fancy being fucked by his big black cock.'

'I think I'll pass up the opportunity at present,' said Marussia thoughtfully, 'though I must say that I have always wondered whether the tales I have heard about Negro prowess and the size of their equipment should be taken with a pinch of salt.'

'Well, I'm no expert on the subject,' replied Nancy, 'but those of my girl friends who have sampled the delights afforded by Standlake's dark, thick tool have been unanimous in their praise of both its dimensions and the way he uses it, which of course is far more important, for, as we say back home, it isn't the size of the ship that counts, it's the motion of the ocean.'

'Still, I would have been most interested to see Standlake in action,' mused Marussia. 'Is there no other way we could see him fuck? Surely he must have some admirers amongst your female staff?'

Nancy clapped her hands in delight. 'Yes, of course, that's the answer – unless Rupert here wishes to take part in a—'

Here I hastened to say that whilst, like the vast majority of public school chaps, I and my best chums Frank Folkestone and Prince Salman of Lockshenstan, had fiddled around with each other after 'lights out' in the dorm, these juvenile experiments were now way behind me. Also, I added, that whilst I had nothing against homosexualists who could do to each other whatever they wished in the privacy of their own homes, frankly, the mere thought of having any prick (let alone a big black one) rammed up my arse was utterly abhorrent to me.

'Don't worry, Rupert, I don't think Standlake is that way inclined either,' Nancy reassured me with a smile. 'Leave this affair to me.'

She called the butler on the house telephone and asked him if he would kindly arrange to fuck one of the maids in his bedroom whilst Countess Marussia and I watched. I could not hear his reply but Nancy nodded her head as she said, 'Yes? Very good, then, we'll go up to Lucy's room in ten minutes.'

Nancy provided us with white towelling robes

to slip on and the three of us made our way back to the drawing-room where we refreshed ourselves with tall glasses of ice cold lemonade which Standlake had thoughtfully left on the sideboard. Then, hardly able to contain our excitement, we went upstairs to Lucy's room which was directly above Nancy's bedroom. When we arrived on the top floor Nancy knocked at the door and her personal maid called out, 'Do come in, everyone, the door is open.'

Standlake and Lucy were already in bed, covered by a sheet but Lucy sat up as Nancy introduced Marussia and myself and we sat down on three chairs that Lucy had placed between the window and the foot of the bed. She was, I must record, a not unattractive girl of some twenty-five years, slightly on the plump side perhaps but blessed with extremely large breasts topped by equally large areoles and rich red nipples which were exposed as she jumped out of bed to greet us. Her mound was covered by a thick profusion of light brown curls and the swelling lips were already pouting most deliciously, the glowing red chink indicating that in all probability Standlake had been frigging her before we arrived.

'Are you ready for me, Philip?' she asked the handsome black man, who grinned, showing two even rows of sparkling white teeth, as he said, 'I should say so, you lucky girl,' and he pointed to the sheet covered peak between his legs. Lucy smacked her lips and threw back the sheet to reveal his naked torso to us. There was a momentary silence and then I heard Marussia gasp in awe at the sight of Standlake's magnificent nude body and I could well understand her admiration for his superb physique. Standlake was, as aforesaid, a handsome fellow, and the muscles fairly rippled as he drew breath and expanded his broad chest. His torso narrowed down to a flat stomach and narrow hips and, as he turned to embrace Lucy, I had also to admire his lean muscular flanks. When he turned back I also gasped with wonder as we caught sight of his heavy, dangling cock which was of such a thickness that I do not believe I have seen before or since.

Marussia was similarly struck by the size of the black butler's boner for the Countess whispered to our hostess, 'My God, Nancy! What an enormous prick! Doesn't the very thought of sucking that huge penis make your mouth water?' And then turning to the girl on the bed whose hands were already encircling this fast-swelling monster, Marussia added, 'You *are* a lucky girl, Lucy. I just hope he doesn't stretch your cunney too much with that giant truncheon.'

'No fear of that, madam, it's only if I take too much of Philip's cock in my mouth that I have any problems, I just can't take it all in without gagging,' said Lucy cheerfully as she leaned over and prepared to begin the demonstration. She took the butler's pulsating dark knob between her lips, jamming down the foreskin and lashing her tongue around the rigid shaft. Then she sucked hard, and amazingly she was able to take about a third of Standlake's extraordinarily thick cock (which at a later date Nancy measured as having a five-and-a-half-inch girth and being fractionally over ten-and-quarter-inches in length) into her mouth whilst her hands toyed with his hanging, heavy balls.

The aroused girl now started to lick this giant dark lollipop, drawing her hot, wet tongue from his ballsack right up to the top of his shaft, fluttering briefly around the uncapped helmet. He clutched at her hair and emitted a low gutteral murmur as she circled her tongue all round the fleshy dome of his knob, paying particular attention, I noted, to the especially sensitive underside.

Then Lucy removed her hands and, clasping them behind her back, she sucked up almost the entire length of Standlake's black prick almost down to the root. This caused the well endowed, handsome Negro to writhe and jerk under this oral stimulation as Lucy sucked up and down his tremendous tadger with noisy abandon. And the clever way she managed to keep her head bobbing up and down without using her hands to steady his twitching tool brought a spontaneous round of applause from Nancy and Marussia, who were still marvelling at the dimensions of Standlake's glistening, veiny boner.

Lucy was obviously enjoying herself for now she transferred her hands back to the front, one clasped as far as her fingers would stretch around Standlake's cock and with the other she was busy diddling herself, rubbing her clitty as she continued to suck on the great stiff staff held lightly between her teeth.

By now we had all reached a fever pitch of

excitement and Nancy was now smoothing her left arm across Marussia's crotch whilst the Countess repaid the compliment by moving her own left hand across to stroke Nancy's breasts. At the same time Nancy reached out with her right hand and with a little help from yours truly, had managed to unbutton my trousers and taken out my own not inconsiderable shaft and her fingers were busying themselves sliding up and down my shiny staff.

Back on the bed, Standlake now had Lucy's head in his hands and was jamming her lips round his cock and I could see that very shortly she would be sucking up all the semen out of his tight, firm balls. In fact, it was only a matter of seconds before the tell-tale quivers and contractions began and Lucy pushed up her head for a moment to allow us to view a great wash of white jism come jetting out of the top of his cock. She slurped up this flood of spunk with evident enthusiasm but to my astonishment, Standlake's proud prick stood as stiff, hard and strong as before he had shot his load!

Indeed, the butler now took control and he leaned forward, his thick lips seeing and finding one of Lucy's engorged nipples, as she now spread herself flat on her back. Once the first tittie had been drawn out to stand up like a little red tap he sucked up the other to a quivering peak of rubbery flesh. Lucy trembled as Standlake moved over her and guided his throbbing tool towards her juicy honeypot and she opened her mouth to take his tongue deep between her moist lips as he now placed his knob at the entrance of her cunney and she pulled her pussey lips apart to widen the entrance for his enormous cock.

I gazed intently as he pushed his prick firmly forward and saw his gleaming pole disappear inch by inch inside Lucy's love channel. Then he began to move it in and out in full yet gentle thrusts as he again attacked her pert little nipples that were standing up, simply begging to be flicked by his long, tapering fingers. To my surprise, Standlake then pulled completely out of her cunney, his black pole gleaming with its coating of pussey juice. But the respite for Lucy's cunt was only temporary – first he lightly traced the open wet crack with his fingertips, flicking the erect clitty that was peeping out at the top, and then he thrust his knob back between those pink, pouting lips and Lucy moaned with delight as he propelled inch after inch of his thick chopper until his rough pubic curls and her muff of smoother pussey hair were matted together.

He pulled back until only his knob was inside her juicy love-channel and then drove the full length of his massive shaft full inside the trembling girl as she urged him on and he quickly established a powerful rhythm whilst Lucy closed her feet together at the small of his back to force even more of that huge stiffstander inside her.

Standlake was now panting with exertion as he rammed his cock in and out of her cunney, his lean black body rocking backwards and forwards between her creamy spread thighs. Lucy was spending as Standlake fucked her for she raked his back with her fingernails as she shuddered with the voluptuous sensations afforded by his thick prick in her voracious cunt. He pumped faster and faster and we three spectators were on our feet, with Nancy's hand still tightly gripped round my own throbbing tool, as we cheered him on. What made the finale even more exciting for us was that Lucy had not been able to find any linseed oil for her *douche* [This was a popular spermicide some hundred years ago though not as effective, of course, as a condom or better still the 'pill' – Editor] so at the very final stage he withdrew and shot a flood of creamy white spunk all over her belly just as Nancy's frigging brought me off and my cock ejaculated an arcing fountain of jism over Standlake's dimpled buttocks.

In fact, I was somewhat concerned, when the butler rolled off the sated girl and lay on his back to recover his senses, that some of my spunk stained the crisp, white sheet. However, when I pointed this out to Nancy she told me not to worry as the cotton was already soaked with Lucy's love juices as well as perspiration from both of the lovers. 'Anyhow, Rupert,' she remarked gaily, 'spunk stains cause no problem if a small amount of Mr Maxwell's Special Compound is used – it is guaranteed to remove all blemishes. We buy a large bottle every month for as you have seen, my friends and I are extremely fond of fucking.'

Countess Marussia looked at her jewel-encrusted pocket watch and said, 'Dear Nancy, I really must be going – I am already late for Lady Suffield's tea party. Thank you so much, my darling, for a divine lunch and a wonderful fuck – for which I must also thank you, Rupert. It was a pleasure meeting you and your nice cock.'

'The pleasure was mine, *simpatichnaya jenshina*,' I replied, bowing low to kiss the Countess's offered hand and using the few words of Russian I remembered from the lessons given me by Dr John O'Connor, the languages master at St Lionel's, one of the most brilliant linguists in England, who was fluent in French, German, Polish, Russian, Turkish and Arabic. Indeeed, if Dr O'Connor had not been caught *in flagrante delicto* with the twin eighteen-year-old daughters of a senior Foreign Office official, he would undoubtedly have enjoyed a distinguished career in the diplomatic service instead of having to earn his daily bread as a humble pedagogue at a minor public school.

'You speak Russian, Rupert? Is there no end to your accomplishments?' laughed Marussia. 'You must take my card. Please call upon me at any time, especially when my consort, Prince Adrian, is back in Amsterdam performing his royal duties.'

We thanked Standlake and Lucy for their wonderful performance and made our way down to the drawing-room. But I stopped at the foot of the stairs and said, 'Nancy, would you object if I popped back upstairs and presented your servants with a small token or our appreciation? After all, they did afford us some excellent sport.'

'By all means,' she replied. 'I am sure they will be far from offended by such a generous gesture.'

'I climbed back up the stairs and as the door of Lucy's room was slightly ajar, I simply strode in. Standlake had already left to shower and change in his own quarters, but Lucy was still lying naked on the sheets, her hands under her head, with a blissful smile of contentment on her pretty face.

'Ah, Lucy, I wanted a quick word,' I said, shutting the door behind me and taking two gold sovereigns out of my pocket. 'On behalf of Countess Marussia and myself, I would like to give you and Standlake a well deserved little present.'

Her eyes lit up as I placed the coins on her bedside table. 'Thank you, sir,' she said, glancing across at the coins and when she saw the glint of gold her eyes sparkled and she sat up and exclaimed, 'Oh, that really is kind of you, sir! I'll give Philip his share later this afternoon.' [Rupert was indeed leaving a very generous gratuity as a housemaid only earned about £30 a year! – Editor]

I was about to leave when the luscious nude girl called me back. 'Must you go, sir? I'd very much like to give you something in return for your generosity.'

Perhaps I was naïve but I honestly didn't know what she had in mind until she crooked her finger and motioned me back to sit next to her on the bed. 'Did you notice the enormous size of Philip's cock, sir?' she asked with a sly smile.

'Yes, I must say that I did, and like most men I was very envious of his tremendous tadger,' I said. This reply made Lucy hold up her hand and say, 'Ah, but honestly, size isn't everything, though I know that all boys would like bigger pricks just as all girls would like an extra few inches on our busts. Now I won't deny that Philip's big stiffie really fills my cunney up a treat but I've known men with much smaller cocks who can bring me off just as well. Lord Hammersmith, for example, is a wonderful lover even though I don't think his bell end is much more than half the size of Philip's – but he reams me out beautifully and his spunk has a fresher, less salty taste too.

'I saw the mistress wanking your cock whilst Philip was fucking me, sir, and I thought that your cock looked very nice. Would you mind if I had a closer look at it?'

'Not in the slightest,' I said, hastily unbuttoning my trousers and pulling out my dangling shaft, 'but as you can see, I am afraid that it's a little bit down in the dumps.'

Lucy clasped my stalk in her fingers and said softly, 'Dear me, we can't let Mr John Thomas stay in this sad state, that's for sure.' She moved herself across and leaned down to place her head on my thigh as I pulled down my trousers and drawers to my ankles. She eyed my cock critically and then moved her hand to pull down the foreskin and expose the naked red bulb of my knob. Her tongue flashed out and slicked across the smooth skin of my uncapped helmet which set my cock swelling up within seconds!

She continued to frig me as she wet her tongue against her lush red lips and then took my knob fully inside her mouth, sucking with gusto as my tool throbbed with pleasure. Sensing that this intense activity would make me spend too soon, she ceased sucking and instead dived her head down to plant a light series of tiny butterfly kisses up and down the stem, encompassing my balls and running beyond to that too often neglected area between the ballsack and arse-hole. She followed this delightful oral massage with some sharp licks on my now bursting shaft and then thrust my trusty tool in and out of her mouth in a quickening rhythm, deep into her throat and then out again with her pink tongue lapping my helmet at the end of each stroke, soaking up the drops of thick liquid which were already forming at the 'eye' on top of my knob. In vain I tried to prolong the delicious pleasure but Lucy's lascivious sucking was simply too powerful to resist and I could not prevent the sperm that had boiled up inside my balls spurting up my stem and crashing out of my pulsating prick.

I pumped a thick, creamy emission of jism inside her mouth which she swallowed with evident delight, smacking her lips as she happily gulped down the last dregs of spunk from my fast-deflating cock. 'Was that nice?' she enquired somewhat unnecessarily. I nodded my head and panted my agreement, 'Lucy, that was a truly splendid sucking-off. Do you know, I've often wondered whether girls can learn how to suck a stiff cock or whether it is simply an inbred ability.'

'I don't really know,' she said, considering my question thoughtfully. 'Perhaps it's something to do with the first time a girl ever takes a cock in her mouth. I remember my introduction to, what's the posh word for it, sir?'

'Fellatio, Lucy,' I answered, as I stole a quick look at my watch.

She must have seen me do so for she continued, 'Oh, please don't go yet, sir. For a start, the mistress will be engaged with Standlake for at least another ten minutes and I'm sure she'd want to say good-bye to you before you leave.'

'Jolly good, then I'll gladly stay and listen to you.' I said, snuggling myself on the bed next to her as she lay with her head on my shoulder and her fingers still toying with my limp shaft.

'Well, it all began three years ago when I left school and took up service in Lord and Lady Jackson's house in Grosvenor Street. It was a very happy household but when her son Terence came back home from Cambridge University for the Christmas holidays, I was silly enough to become intimately involved with him.

'He was a nice, good-looking boy and from the moment he first saw me I could tell that he was as attracted to me as I was to him. Well, it all started one evening when the master and mistress were out at one of Sir Barry Gray's literary soirées in Chelsea. Terry's sister was also out so I knew that he would be alone in the sitting-room. So I marched in there after supper on the pretence of tidying up the newspapers and changing the ashtrays as Lord Jackson smokes those big Cuban cigars. Terry was sitting in an armchair reading the evening paper but I could see him eyeing me over the top of the page as I leaned down in front of him to see if the ashtray on the side table needed emptying. I was wearing a frilly white blouse and I had purposely undone the top two buttons so that the swell of my breasts must have been visible to him. I knew that he would have loved to feel them but, being a polite young gentleman, needed some sign of encouragement before even speaking to me.

'So I deliberately emptied a few grains of cigar ash on his trousers! "Oh, I am sorry, Master Terence, here, I'll brush it off for you," I said, and started to flick away the ash which had landed on his thigh.

'We began to talk and one thing led to another and after about ten minutes I found myself sitting on his lap with my head resting lightly on his shoulder. I was still unsure how to react but then Terry suddenly turned my face up to his and kissed me passionately on the lips.

'I felt a sudden tingling rush of excitement surge through me. There was something so special about his kiss that it made it impossible for me not to respond. His hand slipped down from my shoulder to down underneath my arm and then I felt his fingers close gently over my breast whilst at the same time his tongue sank inside my mouth and his other hand began stroking my thigh under the hem of my skirt.

'Now everything was happening so fast that I didn't even consider trying to resist these unexpected advances. I just sat cuddling him, soaking up the lovely sensations of his kisses and his touches.

'His hand soon reached the top of my legs and his thumb began a delicious stroking of my pussey as I pressed my lips even more firmly against his and his fingers now probed downwards and rubbed against my dampening crack. He then started to tug at my knickers and I lifted my bum off his thighs to allow him to pull them right off. Then I felt my whole body vibrate with pleasure as his thumb rubbed against my clitty and I held on to him as tightly as I could. At that moment, I think we both knew for sure that we wanted to fuck, but as I said, Terry Jackson was a real gentleman because he whispered, "Lucy, before we reach the point of no return, are you certain that you want to make this journey?"

'He need have had no fear for I would have been glad and willing to let him do anything he wanted with my curvy young body. So I simply whimpered when Terry stopped fondling my titties but began undoing the rest of the buttons on my blouse. He slipped it off me completely and then unhooked my chemise and I raised my arms so that he could pull it up and over my shoulders. Now his hands ran firmly over my bare breasts, tracing circles around my stiffening nipples with the tips of his fingers. Then he lowered his head and took one of my erect titties in his mouth and the wet friction of his tongue made it tingle with delight as he sucked it firm and deep between his lips.

'My skirt was next to come off and I was now naked except for my stockings which were held up by two frilly garters. I trembled with desire as he passed a hand over my hairy muff and my cunney was fairly aching for more attention. Yet he still did not attempt to proceed further and it suddenly struck me that Terry might be concerned that I was a virgin! So I nibbled his ear and whispered, "Don't be worried about deflowering me, Master Terry, because in South London where I come from, I don't think there's a girl over sixteen who hasn't had a cock in her cunney at some time or another.''

'This did the trick and I helped him undress until he stood naked in front of me with his thick, stiff cock standing high against his tummy. He stretched me out on the big settee and knelt alongside, kissing my breasts and belly and running his hands up and down my thighs. My excitement grew stronger and stronger and I lovingly clutched at his head of curly brown hair, moaning my approval as he now pressed his mouth onto my bushy mound.

'The sensation of his moist lips felt truly heavenly and when I felt his tongue starting to wash its way around my clitty, I almost fainted away with the sheer ecstasy of the wonderful waves of pleasure which emanated from my cunt and coursed their way through my body. I pushed my pussey up against Terry's face and parted my legs as he now licked even harder at my clitty and at the same time began to prise open my cunney lips with his fingers. He sank his forefinger slowly into my sopping slit, making me gasp as he eased a second and then a third digit deeper and deeper inside my love channel.

'Although I'd been fucked by Mr Hollingberry, our next door neighbour, and by Charlie Haynes and Tim Hutchinson, two boys who lived in the next street, Terry Jackson's wicked tongue and clever fingers were thrilling me like I'd never been thrilled before. My clitty was buzzing with a marvellous feeling which I never before experienced. He twisted his fingers round as he now thrust four fingers in and out of my dripping cunney which made the buzz feel more and more wonderful as he finger fucked me up towards a spend. He realised that my climax was approaching when I began to quiver because he licked harder than ever at my clitty and his fingers raced faster and faster out of my sopping honeypot. When I felt myself on the verge of spending my body jerked wildly but he held his head firmly against my cunney whilst I squeezed my nipples and drummed my feet against the cushions.

'The fabulous pressure of Terry's tongue and fingers kept me at the peak of pleasure for what seemed an incredibly long time – and even when my orgasm finally subsided, I was still feeling very fruity and eager to continue. More than anything, though, I wanted to repay Terry for the gorgeous time he had given me.

'So I urged him to change places and to lie on his back on the settee and I knelt between his legs. His throbbing cock stood up like a flagpole between his thighs and I grasped it with the intention of spitting myself upon the smooth, pink mushroomed knob. But then I remembered that it was not the most propitious time of the month for fucking and anyway I had nothing in my room with which to douche. With a crestfallen look on my face I told him that perhaps I shouldn't let him fuck me after all – this was a terrible thing to have to say for after what had just gone on it was like leading a man dying of thirst in the desert to an oasis and then as he was about to drink warning him that the water was poisoned!

'But Terry did not show any great irritation

with me. He simply stroked my hair and said, "Don't worry, Lucy, I'll be just as happy if you'll suck my cock instead."

'"Of course I will," I said, not wanting to let him know that I had never taken a prick in my mouth before this time. But I'd heard all about how men love being brought off this way and my friend Nellie had told me about how nice it was to lick and lap at a thick prick and how clean and fresh spunk tasted. "It can't get your belly up either, my girl," she had also told me, which was certainly an added attraction as far as I was concerned.

'Nevertheless, the question was whether I would be able to do it well enough for Terry. Now of course, I knew how men liked to be tossed off, and my boy friends had all said that I was very good at giving them hand-jobs, if you'll forgive the expression, sir.

'Anyway, I decided to have a go, and I held the thick base of Terry's prick with one hand and rubbed his shaft up and down with the other as I leaned down and nervously flicked my tongue over the smooth dome of his uncapped helmet. He groaned and lay back with his eyes tightly closed as I repeated this sensual experiment. I must say that I found the sensation of licking his cock much nicer than I'd expected and I could tell from his throbbing tool and his heavy breathing that I must be doing it well.

'Now I gradually eased the crown of his cock into my mouth, nibbling the hot, smooth pole and sucking harder as I moved my hand which had been clutching his shaft downwards to caress his hairy ballsack. I pushed in as much of his thick, rigid rod as I could and for the very first time, sucked and slurped at this lewd lollipop. Terry stretched out his arm and began to frig my cunney as his prick began to twitch and I guessed that the spunk would soon be spouting out. Then with a cry he filled my mouth with a gorgeous spray of frothy warm jism and his shaft bucked wildly as I gulped down all the creamy liquor, which tasted slightly salty but was as pleasant and refreshing to drink as Nellie had told me. I gobbled his jerking prick, rather noisily sucking out every last milky drop of sperm, as Terry's fingers now helped bring me to another voluptuous spend.

'"Was that good for you?" I enquired anxiously, and he smiled up at me. "Lucy, that was truly wonderful," he murmured softly, and would have undoubtedly said more when we heard a ring on the front door bell. I grabbed my clothes and rushed out into the hall and fled upstairs to my room. In fact, the unexpected visitor was only Arthur Barker, an old chum of Terry's who undoubtedly would have loved to have looked on or better still joined in the canoodling. I did come down later at Terry's request and we did enjoy a romp with Arthur along with Jemima, the scullery maid. But that is another story.'

I looked at my watch again and said, 'Lucy, thank you very much for your entertaining little anecdote, but I really must be leaving. Do you think Miss Carrington has finished with Standlake yet?'

'I would imagine so, sir, for as Miss Nancy told me recently, she finds his oversized shaft uncomfortable if it stays too long in her cunney.'

'That doesn't surprise me,' I declared as I began to dress. 'Another time perhaps, you will be able to demonstrate your skills as a *fellatrice* to me.'

Her eyes sparkled as she nodded her head and said, 'I'd love to, Mr Mountjoy. Bring a friend along and I'll show you how I can suck two cocks at once – so long as your friend doesn't have such a giant prick as Standlake!'

I made a mental note of her promise and chuckled as I realised that her *caveat* would rule out my oldest chum Frank Folkestone of whom I had frankly always been a mite jealous as his chopper was by far the biggest amongst all the boys at St Lionel's Academy for the Sons of Gentlefolk [see *The Intimate Memoirs Of An Edwardian Dandy Volume One: Youthful Scandals* and *Volume Two: An Oxford Scholar* – Editor]. It would be an admittedly malicious pleasure to call Frank and tell him sadly that his tool was too large to be sucked off along with my own by this randy young minx.

I bid Lucy good-afternoon and met Nancy at the foot of the stairs. Her face was flushed, her chest was heaving and her clothes were somewhat dishevelled, but she smiled broadly at me and gasped, 'Ah, Rupert, you're just the man I need. Would you allow me to lean on your shoulder as we walk to the drawing-room? I've been really well fucked by Standlake, but I need to lie down for half an hour.'

'Of course,' I said, proferring my arm which

she took in her hands. 'I have also been entertained very nicely by Lucy although I was frankly *hors de combat*. But though I didn't fuck her she told me a lively tale which I will set down in my diary as soon as I get home.

'Nancy, thank you once again for a delicious luncheon and for our post-prandial fun and games. I will telephone you this evening once I have checked my diary and I do hope that you will allow me to return your hospitality.'

We reached the drawing-room and I helped her onto the sofa. 'Phew, that's better,' she exclaimed with a heavy sigh. 'I'll be walking bandy-legged this evening, but I will have no-one but myself to blame. I know I really shouldn't take in Standlake's huge tool after being fucked by another man but my blood was up and as Oscar Wilde said, I can resist anything except temptation!

'Rupert, my dear, I look forward to your call. I am dining with Mr Horne of The Grove Gallery this evening at Romano's so would you telephone before seven o'clock?'

'Yes, I'll call in an hour or so. But how strange you should be meeting Mr Horne tonight. I happened to meet him only last week at my Club where he gave a talk on these new French painters, the post-impressionists, he called them, who have been creating quite a stir on the Continent. Are you in the market for some pictures, Nancy?'

'In a manner of speaking,' she answered, settling herself down on the sofa. 'My father is a keen collector and he has telegraphed five thousand dollars to my bank account in London so I should be able to buy anything that I think he would like.'

'No wonder Garry Horne is taking you out to dinner!' I laughed, as Standlake now appeared with my hat and coat. 'But if you really are looking for some worthwhile paintings, Nancy, I would very much like to show you some work by a very good friend of mine, who used to live very near my own Yorkshire home.'

Then I explained to her about my involvement with Diana Wigmore. I finished by saying that Diana was coming back to England shortly for the important reception given by the local big wigs for the King. Then I had a brainwave and I said, 'Nancy, why not come to York with me and meet Diana for yourself? She has a wide selection of her work at her parents' home and I will telegraph her and tell her to bring some of her latest pictures back with her from Paris.

'You'll stay at Albion Towers, our family seat, of course, and there will be no problem arranging an invitation for you to the party to meet His Majesty. My father is an old chum of the Deputy Lord Lieutenant of the County who is in charge of the whole affair.'

Like all Americans, Nancy was fascinated by royalty and she clapped her hands in delight. 'Gosh, you mean I might meet King Edward himself?' she said excitedly. 'Sure, I'd love to go up to York with you – but I insist on buying the train tickets, especially if I'm to stay at your house. No, Rupert, I won't have it any other way. You have to live on the allowance your Uncle

Humphrey has generously set aside for you whilst I have more money than I know what to do with. Anyhow, Papa can probably use the receipts to offset against his income tax. So when you telephone me in about an hour, give me all the details of the trip.'

I kissed her good-bye and slipped on my hat and coat which Standlake had been patiently holding in his hands. I walked briskly across the Square and as soon as I was home I wrote out a telegraph to Diana telling her that I would definitely be going to York and that I was also writing to her about my plans. Then I scrawled a letter to my father to say that I would come up for the party and that I would be bringing a guest, Miss Nancy Carrington, with me, falsely adding that the relationship between us was strictly platonic because I did not want my Mama to start hearing marriage bells.

Edwards came into the drawing room with a copy of the evening newspaper and I gave him instructions to telegraph my message to Diana immediately and to post my letter to my father. I settled down to read my newspaper but was interrupted by a knock on the door. 'Come in,' I called, and Mary, the pretty maid I had bum-fucked before luncheon, came in and said in a timid voice, 'I'm sorry to trouble you, sir, but I wondered if you would like to have me again this evening. It's my night off and I've nothing to do and nowhere to go.'

'Dear, dear, that's a sorry state of affairs,' I said, folding the paper, and looking up at the demure girl who was standing with her eyes cast down modestly to the floor. 'Though I must say, Mary, how surprised I am that an attractive girl like you hasn't any followers.'

Her face coloured a pretty shade of pink as she said, 'To be honest, Mr Mountjoy, I was going to the music hall with PC Shackleton, but he's been told he has to work an extra shift as three constables at his station are ill with influenza.'

'A policeman's lot is not a happy one,' I said sympathetically, as I hummed the eponymous chorus from the Gilbert and Sullivan opera. 'Still, his loss is my gain. I'd be happy to take you to the music hall, Mary. Where did you want to go?'

'The Alhambra Theatre. Fred Karno's topping the bill,' she said, her face brightening up and her eyes sparkling as she added, 'Oh, you *are* a kind gentleman, sir.'

It was my turn to blush, for my motives were hardly as pure as the driven snow! Although I had already enjoyed what some may call a surfeit of fucking that day, I was never one to turn down the chance of a further frolic. So I said to her, 'It might be a little awkward if we leave the house together, Mary. Why don't we meet at the corner of Gower Street at six o'clock. We'll take in the first house and then we'll have a bite of supper at my Club. But not a word about this to Mrs Harrow or any of the other staff – it'll be our little secret.'

'I won't say a word to anyone, cross my heart,' promised Mary, and she gave me a quick kiss on the cheek before happily scurrying out back to her room. I grinned as I scoured the sports page of the newspaper. To my great joy I read that Fairbridge's Organ had skated home at eight to one in the two o'clock race at Doncaster. Old Goldhill, our family servant back at Albion Towers, who was a keen follower of the sport of kings, had written to me about this horse which was running today in preparation for the Royal Hunt Cup. I had staked a fiver with my Club's head porter who acted as our unofficial bookmaker, so my evening out with Mary would now be doubly pleasing: I could pick up my winnings when we dined at the Jim Jam after the theatre. A seraphic smile creased my lips as it occurred to me that I could fairly claim, after my fol-de-rols with Countess Marussia, a place to ride in the Royal Hunt Cup!

Anyway, I managed to take a quick nap before Edwards brought me tea and sandwiches and after refreshing myself (fucking always gives me an appetite – despite the ample luncheon I was still able to scoff a couple of sandwiches and a pastry), I telephoned Nancy Carrington and we finalised arrangements to go up to York. I also invited her to dine with me next Wednesday evening along with Michael Reynolds, one of my favourite cousins, who being a year older than myself, was already beavering away in his third year as a medical student at the Royal Free Hospital up in Hampstead. Michael was a lusty lad who would appreciate Nancy's liking for free love and I was sure that the girl he was bringing along – a most attractive petite Portugese girl named Shella de Souza, whose soft feminine curves and flashing, lustrous eyes turned men's heads as she walked down the street – would be similarly broad-minded.

There was barely time to shave, shower and change my clothes but at six o'clock on the dot, I carefully descended the front door steps and walked purposefully towards the corner of Bedford Square and Gower Street where I could see Mary was already waiting for me.

Suddenly, the stern words uttered by my father in a private man-to-man talk shortly after my sixteenth birthday crossed my mind. One must never be too intimate with the servants, he had admonished me after seeing Polly the chambermaid leaving my room looking flustered and breathing hard as if she had been running a race – as well she might, incidentally, because the lusty young lass had just ridden a vigorous St George on my stiff cock till I had ejaculated a copious emission of jism up her clinging cunney! My father had gone on to warn me that my behaviour would be bound to lead to problems when the relationship ended, and to be fair, the pater's advice was sensible enough. After all, though I would never simply turn out a girl who became troublesome (especially if she was *enceinte*), on the other hand, as my Indian pal, Prince Salman, used to say, why make problems for yourself in your own home?

But when I caught sight of Mary's pretty face, all thoughts of caution were thrown to the wind. Taking a deep breath, I marched on, and she ran towards me and lifted up her face to be kissed. Arm in arm, we walked down towards Great Russell Street where I hailed a taxi-cab and told the driver to speed us post haste to the Alhambra Theatre.

CHAPTER TWO

On The Town

MARY AND I ARRIVED IN good time for the first house at the Alhambra. Truthfully, I always preferred the second house which was usually noisier and jollier, but this evening, even the first house was crowded, though I did manage to buy two good seats in the fourth row of the *fauteuils* as the front stalls were grandly known.

'I've never sat in the posh half a crown seats before,' said Mary, as she looked up admiringly at the plush velvet curtains which would soon be raised for the first of the evening performances. [These 'posh' seats cost twelve and a half pence each! And even in the Alhambra, one of the smartest of the London halls, a place in the gallery would only cost sixpence. For their hard-earned money, Edwardian music hall audiences were treated to two hours of variety plus a few minutes of jerky Bioscope film 'reproducing the latest events from all parts of the world' – Editor]

We both enjoyed the deft juggling of the talented David Kent (though I inadvertently made Mary choke with giggling when I whispered, 'How on earth does he keep his balls in the air like that?') and we 'oohed' and 'aahed' in amazement at the clever conjuring of the Continental illusionist Simon Barber who produced rabbits out of a hat and white doves out of his inside jacket pockets.

Yet whilst I appreciated the surprisingly clear voice of Seamus O'Toole, a bibulous Irish tenor whose staggering gait convinced me of my initial impression that he was definitely performing in a semi-drunken state, the cloying sentimentality of his songs about lost sweethearts and poor old mothers way back home bored me. But I did perk up after the interval when a twinkling little 'naughty but nice' soubrette named Suzanne Moserre came on and sang *Roly Poly For Mr Moley* and *You Can't Give Mother Any Cockles* and I joined in the choruses with gusto. Fred Karno's troupe acted out a hilariously funny series of sketches and Mary and I laughed till the tears ran down our faces.

After we applauded the company off the stage, I suggested to Mary that we skip the Bioscope and leave before the crush. She agreed and we walked the short distance up through Piccadilly Circus to the Jim Jam Club in Great Windmill Street [a notorious semi-secret rendezvous for Society rakes which is featured in several late Victorian and Edwardian 'underground' journals such as *The Oyster* and *The Memoirs Of Dame Jenny Everleigh*. In his younger days as Prince of Wales, King Edward VII, is known to have attended the extremely raunchy entertainments offered, including dance routines by naked chorus girls and the Club's best-known speciality, the infamous Victor Pudendum contests, about which Rupert will shortly explain – Editor]

I signed Mary in as my guest at the Jim Jam, though I could not help thinking to myself that bringing a girl to the Jim Jam was like bringing coals to Newcastle, for a chap who could not find a female companion at the Club had to be soft in the head – and for good measure, soft in the cock as well! But the reason why I wanted to take Mary to the Jim Jam – though I still feel slightly ashamed about it – was that despite its *louche* reputation, the Club had a strick code of conduct by which its patrons had to abide. For example, all male members who wore a red pocket handkerchief in the top pocket of their jackets or female members who wore a red rose on their dress or in their hair, signified their wish to remain totally *incognito* and would thus not be acknowledged or approached even by their best friends. Needless to say, I was sporting a handkerchief of the brightest red!

'Shall we dine in the restaurant or shall we have supper in one of the private dining-rooms?' I asked Mary, and she immediately plumped for taking our meal in one of the *salles privée*. I ordered whitebait, mulligatawny soup, roast chicken and the chef's fruit compote and whilst we waited for our room to be prepared, we drank glasses of ice-cold white wine. Mary revelled in seeing in person such 'toffs' as Sir Roger Tagholm, Bernard Osborne-Stott, Louis Highgate and all the other men-about-town about whom she had read in the weekly illustrated magazines. 'Do the men only come here to play cards or billiards? They are all walking about unaccompanied,' she remarked, but even before I could answer, her face broke into a sweet, dimpled grin and she said, 'I suppose this is a place where they can meet their sweethearts and make mad passionate love in the upstairs bedrooms.'

I returned her laugh and said, 'You may not be far from the truth, Mary but how did you know there are bedrooms at the Jim Jam?'

'I just guessed as much,' she retorted gaily, 'and Sir Roger Tagholm looks as if he will need one unless the lady he is talking to so intently is a known cock-teaser.'

Looking across the hall I saw Sir Roger engaged in deep conversation with Lady Elizabeth Stompson who was wearing a blue dress with one of the most daring decolletage I have ever seen. Sir Roger, who was a foot taller than Lady Elizabeth, was peering down at the ripe swell of her breasts with undisguised lust as he whispered something in her ear which made her shriek with laughter.

'This is a really ritzy place, Rupert,' said Mary (I had earlier asked her only to address me as 'sir' in the house). 'But what goes on at the Victor Pudendum contest I see advertised on the noticeboard?'

After she had promised not to reveal what I was about to tell her, I explained to Mary that the Victor Pudendum is a contest of elegant fucking that is held monthly in aid of a deserving cause. In this current year, all monies raised would be donated for the Society for Providing Comforts for Poor Families in the East End of London and the total could be quite a substantial sum, the highest being in 1906 when the Club collected £12,500 to send hundreds of slum children to the seaside for a summer holiday.

Quite simply, entrants (who are restricted to Club members or nominated guests at the discretion of the Victor Pudendum Committee) are required to fuck their lovers in front of a specially invited audience. An entrance fee of one hundred guineas per pair was payable together with an extra twenty five guineas if a gentleman preferred to partner a *demimonde* from Mrs Wickley's establishment in Macclesfield Street or Mr Baum's bar just off Soho Square.

The couples were awarded marks for style, grace and originality by a distinguished panel of judges and a gold cup and a purse of two hundred gold sovereigns was presented to the winner of each monthly contest. The entrance fee to watch (which included a bottle of champagne and light refreshments) was twenty pounds for a double ticket and reservations usually had to be made at least two months in advance to ensure getting a table.

'How wonderful,' breathed Mary, who had listened with ever widening eyes to my explanation. 'If you ever fancy entering, do let me be your partner. I'm sure we would do very well and I could certainly make good use of the money if we won!'

A uniformed flunkey sidled up and murmured to me that our room was ready so I escorted Mary up the stairs, nodding to the Prince of Mitten-

Derinen who had beaten me in the second round of the Club lawn tennis tournament held at Hurlingham in July, but who was now coming downstairs with his arm linked with that of a young, buxom blonde who I recognised from the *Daily Mirror* as the winner of the recent national swimming contests held at the Crystal Palace.

The room was tastefully furnished with a table and chairs and also in the darkened corner was a bed with beckoning fluffed up pillows and the sheet invitingly turned back.

But we were now quite hungry and we ate a tasty meal washed down with the fashionable new Buck's Fizz [champagne and orange juice – Editor]. After the waiter had cleared the table, set down a bubbling pot of coffee under a spirit lamp and finally retired, Mary stood up and said, 'Thank you for my lovely supper, Rupert. I've had a splendid time. The only slight problem is that I'm feeling rather warm – would it bother you very much if I took off some of my clothes?'

'Not in the slightest, my dear,' I said, also rising to walk across to the door and lock it. 'As it so happens, I'm also feeling very hot, so if you don't mind I think I'll join you.'

We swiftly stripped to our underclothes and I was clad only in my underpants when, dressed only in her knickers and a slip, Mary sat down next to me on the side of the bed. 'I do hope that Miss Carrington didn't tire you out at lunch-time,' she giggled as she slid her hand in the slit of my drawers to bring out my fast-stiffening cock. 'I've heard what goes on at that house what with the black man and his gigantic prick. Is it really as huge as they say?'

It has always been a source of wonderment to me how one's staff pick up all the gossip which circulates around one's friends and acquaintances. I rather suspect that much of the material one reads about in the columns of the popular newspapers is furnished from paid informants in some of the wealthiest and influential houses [nothing changes! – Editor] – but heaven forbid, if a change in fortune meant that I had to wait upon some of the nincompoops who treat their servants like a lower species of *homo sapiens*.

Nevertheless, I chose my words carefully as I did not want to spread any rumours about Nancy Carrington. 'I did hear that the chap does possess a tremendous whanger,' I said carelessly, 'but size isn't everything, you know.'

'Oh I do agree,' said Mary, running her fingers up and down my now rampant rod which was sticking up like a flagpole out of my undershorts. 'Within reason, my cunney has no problem adjusting to any thickness so long as the cock concerned is hard and stiff. But you men all think that a great big prick will make a girl weak at the knees – and honestly, it ain't necessarily so.'

She cradled my cock in her hand and added, 'Now look at your tadger, Rupert. It isn't the biggest I've ever seen but it's got a nice shape and I like the way it cheekily curves slightly to the left. Mmm, let's see if you've any spunk left in your balls since your lunch, because, despite what you may say, I'm sure that you had a jolly good fuck at Miss Carrington's!'

Her directness acted as a spur and we threw off

our remaining clothes in an ecstasy of abandonment. Our lips met in a passionate kiss which shook us both by its probing, violent tonguing as we explored each other's mouths. Then suddenly she wrenched her lips away and pulled me by my cock onto the bed. Obediently I lay down and then, with a quick smile, Mary's head was between my legs and her hands were clenched around the root of my straining staff. She kissed my knob and washed around it with long swirls of her pink tongue and then the sensual girl brought her mouth down and ran the length of her tongue along the width and length of my shaft, salaciously sucking my throbbing tool, sending waves of sheer, ecstatic pleasure throughout my entire body.

Mary sucked my cock with great relish, cleverly moving her pretty head so that the thrilling sensations ran throughout every last inch of my palpitating prick. At the same time, she smoothed her hand gently underneath my ballsack, lightly grazing the wrinkled, hairy skin with her fingernails. These movements were so exciting that very soon I was trembling with the approach of a searing wave of pleasure which was building up inexorably inside me and my shaft started to shiver uncontrollably as the sweet girl's warm, wet lips continued to encircle my swollen stiffstander.

'I'm coming, Mary, I'm going to shoot my sticky spunk down your throat,' I cried out hoarsely, and this lewd warning seemed to make her suck even more frantically on my quivering cock. The fire flared in my loins and globs of frothy jism spurted out into her receptive mouth. She licked and lapped up my spend, gobbling down my copious emission until I was milked dry.

To our joint delight, my trusty tool was still semi-stiff as I kissed Mary, sinking my tongue inside her mouth and tasting the salty tang of my own spend. I now stroked her cool thighs and she continued to manipulate my shaft which shot back up into a smart erection, pulsating with pleasure at her soft, sensual touch. Now my fingers strayed through her thick auburn curls, tracing their way down the length of her moist crack as she pressed her wet lips even more firmly against mine, clinging to me as tightly as she could, sighing with delight as she soaked up the electric thrills as our melting kisses stimulated us to a fresh round of fucking.

I let my tongue wash over her lips and trace a wet path down to her breasts which I suckled in turn until her rosy nipples were as hard as little red bullets. Mary moaned as we lay writhing naked on the bed and she parted her legs to allow me to run the palm of my hand over the crisp wetness of her open, naked pussey. I raised myself above her and she positioned my cock with her hand, guiding the knob in between the welcoming folds of her cunt.

But then I suddenly remembered what she had told me earlier in the bathroom about this being a bad day for fucking and asking me to go up her bum instead. 'Mary, wait a minute, don't you recall that you said I shouldn't fuck you today?' I gasped, willing myself not to slide my knob home between her cunney lips.

'Yes, but don't worry, when I checked the

calender, I found I had added up the days wrongly. Now's a good time and in any case, I've brought my linseed oil douche with me.' [Linseed oil was a favoured spermicide though not nearly as effective as a condom or 'the pill' – Editor]

Her reply put my mind to rest and so I plunged forward until my cock was embedded to the root in her tingling love sheath. All my senses were now in thrall to her passionate pussey as I pounded my proud prick in and out of her juicy cunt, pushing my cock in as Mary lifted her rear to receive her injection and my ballsack fairly cracked against her arse. She wriggled from side to side as my prick jerked inside her, stimulating every minute part of her tight little honeypot and I could see from the seraphic smile on her face how much she was enjoying this glorious fuck as we rocked furiously towards nirvana.

'Oooh! Oooh! I'm ready, Rupert! I'm ready for your sticky spunk. Fill me up, I want it all!' she hissed through clenched teeth. I jerked my hips as I crashed my cock inside her wonderful cunt one last time before shooting wad after wad of creamy white sperm deep inside her. As my jism splashed against the walls of her womb, Mary's fingernails clawed my back as she spent simultaneously with me and our bodies slapped together as she met each of my violent thrusts with an equally convulsive one of her own and we both screamed aloud with joy as we swam in our mutual love juices, our bodies threshing around wildly until the flow finally slowed and my chastened, shrinking shaft slipped out from the sopping embrace of Mary's love channel.

Gad, what a truly wonderful fuck, though as Mary had to get back to the house before midnight, we had to finish our frolicking after a short rest to recover our composure. However, I shall never forget that hour of lovemaking which, short but sweet, was one of the most passionate I have ever enjoyed.

Before we left the Club I collected my winnings from Bob Cripps, the head porter, who said to me admiringly, 'How on earth did you pick out Fairbridge's Organ, Mr Mountjoy? Did you have some inside information from the stable? I know that Captain Webb in *The Sporting Life* said he was a game little stayer but at best I would only have had a couple of bob each way on a rank outsider in such a strong field. Do you think he's worth backing for the Royal Hunt Cup? Here's your winnings, sir, forty quid exactly. Oh, and when I went round the bookie's to collect, Mr Applebaum asked me to present his compliments and say if you ever wanted to take your business elsewhere, he won't be in the least offended!'

I shrugged my shoulders as I passed the porter five shillings [twenty-five pence – Editor] for his trouble and grinned, 'Hymie Applebaum can't really grumble, Bob, can he? Look how we all came a cropper on Shortbread Biscuit, your friend's tip for the Derby. Remember how Sir Harold Brown had five hundred pounds on the nose and that he had the deuce of a job afterwards placating Mrs Archway and Lady Dyott when it came in one from last because he couldn't afford to take them to Paris for a week which he promised if they'd spend a night in a threesome with him at the Club.

'But as for Fairbridge's Organ, I thought it would be worth having a flutter because I was told the jockey would be trying, Bob, and that's half the battle won in my book. I'm not so sure about the big race, though. It was our old butler back home who tipped me off about the horse so when I see him next month I'll ask his opinion. He knows what he's talking about when it comes to horse-racing and I've often thought that old Goldhill could do much better than Captain Webb and all those other newspaper tipsters. I don't bet very often as you know and one of the reasons is that the horse can't tell me if he fancies his chances. But at least with one of Goldhill's tips, you're not as handicapped as all the other mugs who give their hard-earned money to the bookies.'

'Thank you, sir,' said Cripps, as he saluted me and pocketed his gratuity. 'You're quite right, of course, it is a mug's game. But so long as you don't lose what you really can't afford, I don't think any great harm is done. Mind, some of these idiots who chase their losses by doubling up their bets are crazy and almost deserve to be ruined.'

And with these words of wisdom, the porter hailed a taxi-cab for us and in just ten minutes Mary and I were tip-toeing upstairs to bed. 'You will come into my room when you've finished undressing, won't you?' Mary enquired, and I nodded my assent. 'I should say so, but give me twenty minutes or so as I want to have a shower first,' I said, as I gave her a little kiss, before retiring to my own second floor suite, whilst Mary climbed up to the attic.

I took off my clothes and used the privy before

taking a shower so it was nearer half an hour than twenty minutes before I crept upstairs to Mary's room. There was a soft light flooding out under the door so I knew she was not asleep and indeed I could hear little moans of passion coming from behind her door. Perhaps she was playing with a dildo, I thought, as I opened the door – but in fact, the sounds I had heard had not been coming from Mary but from the throat of young Edwards, the footman, who was sitting on the pretty girl's bed, his head thrown back and his eyes tightly closed and his stiff cock was standing up out of his opened trousers whilst Mary, who was stark naked, was busying herself palating his pulsating prick, running her pink tongue up and down the not inconsiderable shaft.

When she lifted her eyes and saw me standing there she lifted her head and murmured, 'Eddie, Mr Rupert's arrived, we can begin our fun in earnest now,' and then the bold miss looked up to me and said, 'I thought you'd like something a little different to end the evening. To start with, would you like to see Eddie fuck me? Perhaps you could tell us if we're good enough to enter this Victor Pudendum contest at the Jim Jam Club you were telling me about. It would be great fun and absolutely marvellous if we actually won – Eddie needs some more money to help his brother who is an apprentice carpenter and doesn't earn very much and God knows, my family are always broke.'

Frankly I was none too pleased at her little speech because Mary knew full well that I did not want any news of our evening out to filter through to the other servants. But she must have read my mind because she added, 'Oh, I know you wanted everything kept secret, sir, but don't worry. I wouldn't have mentioned a word to Eddie if I didn't know he could keep mum. I mean to say, he wouldn't get a reference if he ever split, would he, and I wouldn't ever let him in my cunney again.'

'She's right, sir,' said Edwards, nodding his head. 'Honestly, I'll be as silent as the grave. Colonel Wright knew I could be trusted and often asked me to poke one of the ladies he brought home if they were feeling randy and he was too tired to oblige.'

Well, at first I wasn't very keen at the prospect of sharing Mary with anybody, let alone a lowly footman, though this unworthy sentiment (for I am sure that the chap who cleans out the public conveniences at Oxford Circus is probably a more considerate bed-mate than some aristocratic toffee-nosed chump like Lord Slough whose unspeakable behaviour towards Miss Nellie Colchester led to his expulsion from the Jim Jam Club) soon passed, as I've always enjoyed an erotic exhibition – especially when I know that I will have an opportunity to join in if I so desire, and so I pulled up a chair and told the couple to proceed. If nothing else, it would be interesting to compare them to Standlake, Nancy Carrington's big-cocked black butler, and Lucy, her attractive and articulate maid.

Mary began by feeling for Edwards' prick which had shrivelled up and sunk back inside his drawers. She moved her hand up and down, giving his shaft a few vigorous rubs and then brought out his now stiffened shaft. Then she lowered her lips to kiss the uncapped knob but after a quick lick or two she lifted her head and said, 'Eddie, I think we'll do far better if you undress first.'

He swiftly shed his clothes and stood up as Mary ran her hands across his broad, hairy chest and then slid them down to grasp his thick, hard cock which was standing up to attention almost flat up against his belly. She then knelt down to take his cock inside her mouth, pushing out the cheeks of her bum to afford me a truly excellent view of both her cunt and arse-hole. This exciting sight made my own cock swell up to a throbbing stiffness and I could barely restrain myself from tearing open my trousers and frigging off then and there.

Mother Nature never ceases to amaze, for somehow Mary managed to take the whole of Edwards' bursting shaft between her lips. Then the libidinous little minx started to suck this giant pink lollipop, moving her head to and fro so that his cock moved smoothly back and forth though she took care that his knob was always engulfed inside her wet, warm mouth. Meanwhile, she juggled his balls gently through their hairy, wrinkled covering until she opened her mouth and whispered to him to lie down on the bed. He obeyed without demur and lay flat on his back, his rampant stiffstander sticking up as firmly as an iron bar under Mary's deft handling.

She then rose up, still clenching his cock in her hand and turned her peachy bum cheeks to me as she straddled him and inserted his knob between her pussey lips which I could see pouting out amidst her curly muff. Slowly she lowered herself upon his veiny shaft until she was sitting on his upper thighs with every last inch of cock crammed inside her dripping honeypot. They stayed motionless for a few moments as in a *tableau vivant*, enjoying to the full the mutual sensations of repletion and possession, so delightful to each of the players of this most glorious sport afforded us by our beneficient Creator.

Soon it was time, however, to commence those soul-stirring movements which lead inexorably to the grand finale of frenetic fucking. I wriggled in my chair as I heard the squelchy sound of Mary's cunney sliding up and down Edwards' thick shaft and I licked my lips as I saw the gorgeous girl rub her titties as she drove down hard with a delighted squeal, spearing herself on his glistening tool until the lusty pair melted into a delicious state of ecstasy. They came together with great cries of release as Edwards shot a great gushing stream of spunk up her cunt mingling with Mary's own love juices which were running out of her love channel and soaking Edwards' pubic bush.

The footman swung himself out from under her gleaming, ripe young body and he was so intoxicated by the force of his spend that he rolled over too quickly and went crashing down onto the floor. Mary giggled as she looked over the bed and Edwards groaned but luckily he was unhurt though naturally a little shocked by his fall. She threw him a pillow which he tucked under his head as he gasped, 'Phew, what a great fuck! But you must both forgive me – I'm absolutely done in and I just must grab forty winks.'

'Don't worry about it, Edwards, we'll wake you up when we need you,' I cried and within a few seconds I could see his eyes close and his chest heave up and down as he sank directly into the arms of Morpheus. Of course, I was more than happy at his being *hors de combat* as, despite what my father disparagingly calls my egalitarian notions, I had no desire whatsoever to fuck in front of my well-endowed footman. Anyhow, I tore off my clothes and Mary jumped out of bed and stood stark naked in front of me as we embraced, standing belly to belly, with nothing between us except my thick, throbbing tool which was being delightfully squeezed between our tummies.

She grabbed hold of my prick and inspected my cock closely. 'You are lucky to have such a nice-looking cock, Rupert,' she said admiringly. 'It fits so nicely in my cunt, I really couldn't ask for more. It's one of the thickest I've had for some time too.'

'You're just saying that to flatter me,' I laughed, but she shook her mop of dark shiny hair. 'No, I mean it, really I do,' she insisted. 'Why, it's thicker than Eddie's for a start.'

I looked at her in disbelief but she squeezed my shaft again and said, 'It is, honest it is! You know, the trouble is that you can only see your cock when you look straight down at it whereas when, say, you see another gentleman's prick in the changing room, you're seeing it from a different angle which makes it look bigger.

'I heard Colonel Wright say that at a dinner party after the ladies had retired and I was helping Eddie clear the table,' she said with some satisfaction. 'It's so obvious when you stop and think about it.'

I couldn't help laughing as I hugged her tightly and then inclined her backwards until we fell upon the bed and we lay at full length, side by side but with my head by her calves, both of us as eager as could be to enjoy a good *soixante-neuf* to start the ball rolling. I began the programme by burying my head between her thighs and I inserted the tip of my tongue into her inviting little crack, sucking up the remains of her previous spend, making Mary writhe with passion as she pulled her face up to my prick and murmured, 'Let me honour His Highness with a twenty lick tonguing,' as she slipped my ruby knob inside her mouth. She worked on my helmet for a while and then bobbed her head in rhythm as she lapped at my trembling tool with great long licks from the base to the top which almost drove me insane with desire.

I was so aroused that I stopped nibbling at her erect little clitty and panted, 'Careful now, Mary, or I'll come too quickly, and that will never do.' She heeded my warning and scrambled round to lie flat on her back with her legs wide open. Naturally, I took my cue from her blatant posture and grasped my cock, giving it a quick rub before feeding into her juicy cunt. Without undue haste, I slid my knob between her pink pussey lips and inched my shaft inside her willing cunney. Then, once I was fully embedded, I started to fuck her with long, smooth strokes and we laughed merrily as I hovered above her, supporting myself on my arms. My balls slapped in slow cadence on her buttocks as I moved down, up and down again, increasing the pace as I thrust in with intensity until the voluptuous girl was squealing with joy.

As I approached the heights, I changed the tempo of my fucking to one of swift, short jabs. Mary rotated her bum cheeks as I pulsed in and out of her squelchy cunt. I climaxed first, my quivering cock squirting out jets of creamy jism and very soon afterwards Mary followed me over the top to a huge, shuddering orgasm. Luckily, my cock remained stiff for Mary's blood was on fire and she immediately wriggled over and thrust out her proud curvey backside at me. Nothing loath, I now proceeded to fuck her doggie-fashion, gripping her hips and sliding my still rampant rod between her bum cheeks and into her pussey. I fucked away with all the energy I could muster, the throbbing and contraction of her cunney muscles on my enraptured cock spurred me to even greater efforts until with a cry of triumph I pumped a second stream of boiling spunk inside her. This exhausting exercise made me dizzy with fatigue and I collapsed down beside her in an untidy heap whilst Mary rolled over and kissed my cheek with a warm smile of satisfaction on her lips.

By the time I had recovered, Edwards had woken up from his intense slumber and at Mary's invitation, had squeezed himself onto the bed. There wasn't enough room to lie down so we sat on the side of the mattress with Mary in between us. By Jiminy! This randy girl was really insatiable! In no time at all she had taken our two naked cocks in her sweet grasp and following her directions, Edwards held one taut tittie and I held the other and we squeezed and rubbed them as she squirmed with pleasure, holding on to our pricks all the while as she frigged our tools delightfully.

Mary was so aroused by this lewd scenario that she climaxed before either Edwards or I had squirted our spunk and so we waited impatiently to take our further orders from this lusty mistress of ceremonies. She took little time in deciding what she wanted, sliding back onto the pillow and demanding that Edwards tittie fuck her. He clambered over her and she cushioned his cock in the valley between her ample bosoms. The footman began sliding his shaft between them as she called out for me to pay homage to her cunney. So I knelt down between her legs and she wrapped her thighs around my neck as I buried my face in her curly thatch of black pussey hair. I kissed her salivating cunney lips and started by licking her slit in long lascivious swipes. The vermilion love lips soon turned red and parted and between them I felt for her stiff little clitty which I rolled around in my mouth.

'Ohhh! Ooooh! OOOH!' she yelped as I nibbled the edges of her clitty with my teeth. 'Suck harder, Rupert, suck harder and make me come!'

How could I disobey such a sweet command? I

sucked and slurped with renewed vigour, rolling my tongue round and round her love button, lapping up the aromatic love juice which was now flowing freely from Mary's juicy honeypot. Her whole body stiffened as she felt an oncoming orgasm and then her hips bucked violently, her back rippled and from her cunney there spurted a fine creamy emission, which flooded my mouth with its milky essence, that I swallowed down until Mary shuddered into limpness as her delicious crises melted away.

Meanwhile, Edwards' cock was still being massaged between the soft globes of Mary's breasts. The sight of his throbbing boner slewing its way back and forth stimulated her so much that she pulled his bottom cheeks towards her until his prick was above her face and she popped the hot staff inside her mouth. I could see her tongue work up and down, licking the entire length of his tadger, taking playful little nips at the sensitive tube of cockflesh, and when she realised that he was about to spend, her hands flew up to his balls and, smoothing her hands over them, she gulped down the copious emission of jism which poured out from the young footman's twitching tool.

I dived down to kiss her pussey once again and instinctively she opened her legs to make the swollen love lips more accessible. My tongue moved, delving, probing, sliding from the top of her sopping crack to the base of her cunney-hole, my tongue lapping up the tangy cunt juice which was cascading out of her pussey.

Then I stiffened the tip of my tongue and

started to lick the soft, puffy inner lips and I eagerly inhaled the fresh zephyr of feminine aroma which arose from her and I made her moan with ecstasy as I pushed the tip of my tongue deep into Mary's love channel. Her hips were gyrating wildly as I stroked my tongue in and out of her and I licked her rhythmically up and down, delighting in the feel of the swollen flesh pulsing in eager response. Her clitty grew harder each time my tongue flicked across it, jerking and rising up to meet my wicked little laps. I moved my head up to concentrate on her clitty and I must say how much I loved the way it grew like an excited miniature penis as I tickled it with my tongue. I continued to tease it, driving her wild with slow, firm strokes until she fairly screamed out, 'Fuck me, Rupert, please fuck me! I must have your big cock inside my cunt!'

I gave her cunney a final *au revoir* kiss and flipped the quivering girl over to fuck her doggie-style. This greatly appealed to her for she stuck her rounded backside high in the air and reached back to fondle my balls as I parted her bum cheeks and pushed my prick into her drenched, welcoming cunney. Holding on to her delicious bottom I began pounding in and out of her cunt with long, deep strokes, raising the tempo from *lento* to *andante* and building up to an inevitable *furioso*. She squealed delightedly and yelled out, 'Now! Now! Shoot your spunk up my pussey, you randy rascal!'

I was ready to oblige as I could already feel the first pulsations of an oncoming spend as the jism started to boil up in my balls though I hung on for as long as possible, drawing out the joust to a thumping climax. My sinewy cock slewed a passage through her tingling cunney and Mary was tearing at the sheets and moaning into the pillow as with a final heave I coated her cunt with a fine spurt of sticky sperm as together, we rode the wind . . .

The three of us licked and lapped, sucked and fucked until the first rays of the morning sun lit up Mary's bedroom. I hastily threw on my clothes and said to the two servants, 'Mary, tell Mrs Harrow that you are suffering from a severe headache. Edwards, you'll have to rise up at the usual time, I'm afraid, but don't come in and wake me. Now I will be going out after breakfast and I won't need your services until I return this evening. You can also tell Mrs Harrow that you feel unwell and that you will also have to retire to bed. The good lady will assume that you and Mary have both caught the same germ and will not question either of you too closely.

'However, to be fair to the rest of the staff, I would suggest that you both get up by about two o'clock to help out with any remaining domestic duties.'

They thanked me for proposing this kind stratagem and quietly I made my way back to my room and fell into a deep sleep from which I did not wake until almost ten o'clock. As I washed and shaved it occured to me that I had really been foolish to fuck with my footman and chambermaid. I might be able to trust Mary but as the old saying goes, no man is a hero to his valet, though it would be shockingly unfair to dismiss

Edwards who had done nothing dishonourable.

Well, it would all depend on his behaviour when I sat down to breakfast. Would he be arch? Would he be familiar? Or would he put on airs? Perhaps he wouldn't even come in with the newspaper and the post. But thank goodness, all my worries were unfounded, for Edwards greeted me with his usual deferential 'good-morning, sir,' as he passed me the *Daily News* and the single letter which had arrived earlier in the morning.

A lucky escape, nevertheless, I mused, and resolved never to repeat the mistake as I read the short note addressed to me by Henry Bascombe-Thomas, an old chum from St Lionel's Academy, who I had not seen for a year – since after leaving Cambridge University, he had decided to cross the Atlantic and spend a year in America, studying modern art under Professor Sidney Cohen of New York University.

Henry was an artistic cove, much given to writing occasionally good verse, painting some rather rum pictures and wearing his hair far too long for our headmaster, Dr Keeleigh's taste. Some foolish fellows at St Lionel's wrongly assumed that Henry was a woofter [homosexual – Editor] and soon found out that though of an eminently peaceful disposition, if pushed too far, Henry could also deliver an uppercut to the jaw, though like myself, he abhorred physical violence and refused (again like myself) to be considered for the school boxing team.

I should add that like a surprising number of very clever chaps, Henry was terribly absent-minded – which explained why his letter to me arrived a full two days after he had posted it from Southampton as he had addressed it to Bedford Street instead of Bedford Square. However, no harm had come from the delay as you will see, dear reader, from this copy of his message which I had deciphered with no little difficulty from his unreadable scrawl. It read as follows:

Dear Rupert,

I returned to England last week on the SS Shmockle, *the flagship of the Hanseatic Line owned by Count Gewirtz of Galicia who happened to be on board. The weather was inclement for the first two days but all in all I had a most enjoyable journey which I'll tell you about when we meet.*

Could we lunch on October 29 at the Jim Jam? I'm on my way to Chichester this afternoon to see my parents but I'll be coming up to town tomorrow evening and staying at the Jim Jam for a week till I find myself some rooms. Unless I hear from you (you can telegraph me at The Old Vicarage, Mackswell Avenue, Kendall, Near Chichester), I'll assume you can make it. Shall we say one o'clock in the first floor bar?

Looking forward immensely to seeing you again,
Henry

Now I had planned a semi-artistic kind of day myself. This would have started with a brisk stroll down to Holywell Street to see the new prints from Paris at the Birmingham Gallery where Mr Malcolm Campbell owns the largest selection of erotic pictures in the country, kept under lock and key away from the general public and shown only for viewing by selected customers. Afterwards, I would have hailed a cab to Pall Mall to take luncheon followed by an afternoon snooze at The National Reform, one of my more respectable clubs.

However, even though I had spent some time at the Jim Jam the previous evening with Mary, I wanted to see Henry again and hear all his news. So I decided to postpone my visit to the Birmingham Gallery to another day and instead I thought I would spend a quiet morning browsing amongst Colonel Wright's bookshelves as my landlord was an avid reader and collector of first editions. There was little of interest in the newspaper, so after demolishing a bowl of porridge, a full plate of bacon, eggs, sausages and five slices of buttered toast, I took my third cup of tea into the library and scoured the shelves for something interesting to read.

By pure chance I pulled out a book titled *Modern Women* and opening it to the title page I read that this leather bound tome was of 'conversations with various girls in Belgravia and Mayfair' by a Mr Oliver Dunstable, an author whose writing was hitherto unknown to me. There was, however, a preface written by none other than Sir Rodney Burbeck, one of the gayest Lotharios in London. He had written: *'This fresh and original book gives us an excellent verbal picture of what today's men and women are thinking and what they want from their counterparts. There is a perception and a sense of humour in his writing which makes Mr Dunstable not only delightful to read but well worth thinking about afterwards. The illustrations consist of portraits which will be recognised at once by anyone familiar with current members of Society.'*

This was praise indeed! And from such a source as Sir Rodney, it surely heralded some gallant writing, which always afforded me the greatest enjoyment. So I settled down with a glow of anticipation on my face as I read Mr Dunstable's account of his interview with Melissa Rotherwick, perhaps the prettiest of all the debutantes who 'came out' in 1905, who I remembered meeting at Lord Bresslaw's Autumn Ball last year. She was one of the most beautiful young women one could wish to see, with gold-dusted light-brown hair, expressive large eyes, rich ruby lips and pearly white teeth.

Mr Dunstable had had the good fortune to meet her at the splendid country mansion of Stockleigh Hall, her family country seat down in Kent and she talked openly of her belief that further education should be given to young people about matters appertaining to *l'art de faire l'amour*.

As this book was printed privately, I doubt if many readers will be acquainted with Melissa's frank account of how she and her schoolfriends were forced to kidnap, if this is not too strong a term, a willing young man, so as to find out for themselves the joys of a good fuck. Therefore I propose to bring her words to a wider audience by reproducing them here. The uninhibited young girl was telling Mr Dunstable of her years spent at Mrs Bartholomew's Boarding School For Young Ladies not far from Redstock at the foot of the Mendip Hills.

Melissa Rotherwick told Mr Dunstable: *It will be readily understood, I am sure, that being all of the same sex, we found it most frustrating to be shut up in a friendly but strictly enclosed establishment in the heart of Somerset without a single member of the male species to be found anywhere on the premises with the exception of our chaplain, Reverend Jonathan Crawford, a nice old gentleman of seventy-three who conducted services every Sunday morning in the school chapel.*

As may be readily imagined, we were forced to explore amongst ourselves, so to speak, for our private pleasures and it was hardly surprising that there were many close, emotional ties which flourished between the young ladies.

However by the time my pals and I had reached the dizzy heights of the sixth form, such juvenile 'pashes', as we called these intra-feminine love affairs, had palled and we were ripe for plucking by any lucky young man who might come our way. But we were so strictly chaperoned away from anything masculine (even the school cat was a plump ginger tabby!) that it seemed we would never be able to sample the fruits of sensual passion until we had left Mrs Bartholomew's custody.

Yet despite these restrictions, as the old saw has it, love laughs at locksmiths, and in the course of time a day dawned when some of us were able to put the theoretical knowledge we had gained from the copy of Dr Nigel Andrews' Fucking For Beginners, which my friend Annabel had smuggled into school after borrowing the copy she found in her brother's room during a Christmas vacation, to a most pleasant practical use.

This event happened by a series of fortunate circumstances and involved George Cox, the aptly named young nephew of Reverend Crawford, who was spending a few days down in Somerset visiting his elderly relation. But first I had better explain that at Mrs Bartholomew's, one of the benefits of seniority was that on Wednesday afternoons members of the upper sixth form were allowed out of bounds to stroll unaccompanied along the path, through Farmer Trippett's meadow, down to the banks of the small stream which ran between his fields.

Well, one fine spring afternoon, during my penultimate term at the school, my friends Annabel and Sheena accompanied me for a walk along this path and we were discussing some abstruse mathematical problem which had been set that morning by Mrs Bartholomew herself. I must give my old head teacher due credit at this point and record the fact that science and mathematics played major roles in our curriculum, unlike the majority of similar academies for young ladies where only the arts are studied in any serious way. Anyway, we were deeply engrossed in this rather learned conversation when Annabel suddenly stopped talking and I saw her jaw drop and her mouth hang open as she stood stock still, staring across to the far bank of the stream.

Sheena and I followed her gaze and we were also struck dumb by what we saw – for lying flat on his back, fast asleep, was none other than George Cox, who had obviously taken a dip in the river and followed it by a luncheon of sandwiches and the best part of a bottle of white wine which lay beside in an ice-box. This in itself would not have been such an extraordinary sight but for the fact that George had divested himself of his clothes for his swim and had not bothered to put them back on again afterwards, thinking no doubt that as he was on private land, no-one would be coming by! So there he lay, naked as nature intended, and for the first time in our lives, we three girls were given the opportunity to look at a full-sized genuine penis.

Frankly, at first sight, this squashed up tube of flesh which protruded out of a growth of mossy pubic hair and lay limp over George's thigh did not impress us.

'It doesn't seem nearly as big as the pricks shown in Fucking for Beginners,*' commented Sheena, and Annabel agreed with her, saying that the dildo she had purloined from her sister was also of a greater length and girth.*

'Wait a moment though, girls,' I said to them. 'Surely we must only compare like with like and so we mustn't pass judgement upon George's cock until we've actually seen it standing up to attention. You may recall that Dr Andrews wrote in Chapter Three about the vast majority of cocks all swelling up to about the same size even though some look bigger than others when simply dangling between men's legs.'

Annabel nodded sagely and said, 'Yes, I think you are absolutely right, Melissa, but experientia docet, *as Miss Bartholomew would doubtless say. I suggest that we find out exactly what a stiff prick actually looks like for ourselves. I'm sure that George won't mind. He's fast asleep anyhow and if we keep very quiet, we might be able to play with his cock without waking him up.'*

This sounded like an extremely sensible course of action to me and Sheena also agreed to take part in this voyage of sensual discovery. So we slipped quietly over the ramshackle wooden bridge and sat ourselves carefully round George who was still apparently fast asleep. Boldly, Annabel took hold of his soft shaft whilst I tenderly lay my palm underneath the hairy, wrinkled ballsack underneath it.

Thanks to our careful perusal of Dr Andrews'

valuable tome, we were not too alarmed when George's tool stirred as Annabel clutched it in her fist and began to swell and thicken. Sheena now entered the fray by drawing back the skin at the top to reveal a smooth pink mushroom shaped knob. I withdrew my hand from George's ballsack which had tightened up as his prick had begun to grow and ran my fingers round it as well. I was fascinated by the feel of this, my first naked cock, which felt like an ivory column covered in warm velvet.

'It looks far better now,' Annabel commented with all the satisfaction of having been proved right. With a glint in her eyes Sheena said, 'George has a very pretty prick indeed and the way it throbs when I touch it is making me tingle all over.'

Her words made me aware that I was also experiencing a buzz of excitement throughout my body. My titties were as hard as two little rubbery nuts, my legs were trembling and my pussey was throbbing with the same kind of urgency I experienced when playing with myself, only stronger and more insistent. A novel thought then entered my head and I said to my companions, 'I wonder whether this cock tastes as good as it looks,' and I kissed the very tip of the smooth dome of the uncapped helmet. Remembering what I had read in Dr Andrews' book, I licked round the knob and then I opened my lips and inch by inch, took the throbbing tool in my mouth. As my lips gently slipped further and further down its length, I sucked and pulled at the hot, hard shaft with my lips and I noticed that Annabel had now slipped her hands under George's ballsack and was very carefully caressing his testes.

It was at this stage that George's eyes began to flutter open and he looked on in amazement as I continued to palate his prick whilst Annabel now busied herself by licking his balls. 'I must be dreaming,' he muttered and struck himself a sharp blow on the cheek.

'No, I'm awake all right,' he said aloud, trying to reassure himself that he had not taken leave of his senses. 'This is really happening. To the best of my knowledge I'm not simply the victim of a delicious hallucination. It's still Wednesday afternoon and I have just woken up after falling asleep after lunch and now I find I'm being sucked off by two beautiful girls from Mrs Bartholomew's school.'

Poor George may have been dreadfully puzzled but he was no fool and with a contented sigh he decided not to tempt providence by asking further questions and simply laid back to enjoy the exquisite sensations of the soft, wet lips and tongues running over his cock and balls. 'A-a-a-h!' he gasped and he shot a jet of frothy creamy essence into my mouth. Instinctively I swallowed his sticky emission and though a tad too salty for my taste, I knew it would not harm me, for as our mentor Dr Andrews noted, fresh semen is highly nutritive. [Indeed it is, as it contains substantial amounts of vitamins and some traces of zinc and nickel – Editor]

However, as the good doctor also said, the tang may vary from man to man, which made me resolve to have another suck, preferably of another meaty specimen, for whilst I much enjoyed milking George's member, I wanted to try out the flavour of other suitable young men, for as Dr Andrews commented, the flavour of spunk is an acquired taste which often takes a little time to appreciate.

But meanwhile Sheena now demanded a turn to gobble George's prick and the dear lad kindly proffered his limp shaft without hesitation saying only that he would appreciate a few minutes' recuperation from the prodigious spend of seed caused by my own superb sucking of his cock.

To help revive his crestfallen member I told George to get up on his knees in front of me as I lay back and parted my legs to give him a wonderful view of my furry thatch and pink cunney lips. I took his hand and placed it on my already dampening mound. 'Oh my what a truly beautiful cunt,' he breathed, as the fingers of his left hand splayed my outer lips and the fingers of his right ran up and down the length of my love slit. Gently, he inserted his forefinger between my pussey lips and my hips rose up to greet the welcome visitor.

He finger-fucked me for a little while but soon his head dived down between my thighs and I was in raptures as he found my excitable little clitty and my pussey started to spend freely under the voluptuous titillations of the randy youth's velvety tongue. I clasped my legs around his head as he licked and lapped on my tingling cunney and I screamed with joy as I quickly reached the pinnacle of sensual delights.

I released George's head from between my crossed legs and Annabel and Sheena pushed him flat on his back and he obeyed with alacrity their command to lie quite still. Sheena smoothed her hand over his flat stomach and let her fingers wander into his thick growth of pubic curls. She licked her lips with gusto as she gazed down upon his thickening shaft that was not yet fully erect but which had a lovely, heavy look about it. She grasped the swelling staff in her hand and gently squeezed it – and immediately George's cock stood up in full, glorious erection, his rosy helmet now bared as Sheena helped snap back the covering foreskin. Her lips now swooped down and she began to kiss and lick the red mushroomed knob, dwelling around the ridged edge and moving slowly up and down the underside before sucking in as much of the shaft as possible into her mouth. She frigged his prick firmly with her fingers, licking and lapping, as she clamped her lips over his cock, sucking furiously until she was forced to release it as she felt she was in imminent danger of choking.

Whilst this was taking place, I was fingering myself, opening up my pussey even further and, when George withdrew from Sheena's mouth, I reached up and pulled his glistening, wet cock towards my aching cunt. Then, as if I had been doing this all my life, I raised my legs and grasped him round the waist and for the first time savoured the indescribably delicious feeling of my cunt being filled with a real live prick slewing a path backwards and forwards as he began to fuck me in earnest.

Of course, my hymen had long ago been broken by a combination of horse-riding and frigging with friends and the aid of a dildo, so there was no pain but only a most delightful pleasure as George's cock pistoned deep inside my cunney and then slid back to repeat the effort. Also, I could lie back and enjoy my first fuck without worry as my monthies were due within forty eight hours. [Hardly infallible reasoning but certainly this is a most unlikely time in the cycle for any unwanted consequences – Editor]

By now my body was responding as if by instinct and I was thrusting my hips up to meet him time and time again. I responded with vigour, now carried away totally as he rubbed my titties whilst his sinewy rod crashed its way through my sopping love channel. Then my back arched and I realised in one unforgettable instant that for the first time in my life I was spending with a man's cock inside me . . .

Suffice it to say that I came and I came and I came and when at last George's prick quivered and spurted a sticky libation of spunk inside me I was so overcome that I almost swooned with ecstatic joy. George too was similarly overcome and collapsed on top of me as I lay heaving and panting whilst the last waves of this gigantic spend washed over me.

So ended my first fuck. Annabel and Sheena kindly helped me dress and we arranged to smuggle George into our dormitory that very evening for some further fun and games. Annabel also had the brilliant idea of asking George to bring a friend with him if he possibly could, as even such a stout hearted and well-endowed cocksman as he could not hope to satisfy six lusty young maidens. As luck would have it, his old school chum, Clive Hampstead (who later became renowned for his abilities to perform cunnilingus, until his marriage to a wealthy American heiress led him to settle in Chicago), lived not five miles away and was happy to join us in a riotous night of sucking and fucking about which I cannot tell you as at least one of the girls concerned is now the wife of a very important personage indeed and she would be horrified if her participation in this orgy of sensuality was ever made public.

I closed the book and stood up with a raging hard-on as I thought about how divine it would be to fuck the gorgeous Melissa Rotherwick who, as one could gauge from this graphic account of her first fuck, was obviously a generous and free-spirited girl. I made a mental note to check if by any chance her name appeared on the members' list of the Jim Jam Club before I met

Henry Bascombe-Thomas there for luncheon.

Reluctantly I decided against summoning Mary to be fucked or at least to frig or suck off my uncomfortably stiff cock. It was not only my earlier resolve to cease fucking servant girls which kept my thumb away from the bell, but also the thought that it would be sensible to give my prick a rest in case Henry and I were offered invitations to one of the wild private parties which certain ladies had taken to holding at the Club on weekday afternoons.

So I walked slowly round the room three times, emptying my mind of everything, except the question of how many books might be stacked on the shelves of this well-stocked library. In time, my attempt to solve this problem by assessing the approximate number of books on one average shelf and multiplying this figure by the number of shelves did the trick and my rampant stiffstander slowly subsided. I went into the hall and called Edwards to say that I would probably return around five o'clock but in the unlikely case of needing to speak to me urgently, he could contact me at the Jim Jam Club whose telephone number I scribbled on a sheet of paper and pressed into his hand.

Now as the rain which had pattered down earlier in the morning had subsided and enough patches of blue were visible through the clouds, I had planned to walk down to Great Windmill Street – but just as I strode away from the front door, a carriage drawn by two smartly attired black horses pulled up alongside me and a familiar voice called out to me. 'Hello there, young Rupert, can I give you a lift?'

I looked round to see the occupant of the carriage throw open the door. I walked across and squinted inside to see if I had correctly identified the owner of the rather fruity tones. And yes, I was right, for leaning against the expensive kid leather upholstery was the portly figure of Colonel Stanley Gooner formerly of the Ninth Punjab Rifles, a former comrade-in-arms of my father and one of my parents' oldest friends.

The Colonel, in his early days, had won an award for gallantry whilst serving on the North West frontier in an incident that made headlines in the popular newspapers. After his patrol had been ambushed by the Pathans, he escaped, but returned dressed in the clothes of a native woman and in an audacious single-handed operation, he managed to rescue two captured colleagues whose pricks were about to be amputated (without even the benefit of anaesthetic) by a mob of angry Afghans. I am hazy as to exactly how he managed to place a pistol against the balls of the much-feared enemy commander, a bandit notorious for his brutality, but the stratagem worked and the then Captain Gooner was able to bargain successfully for the freedom of the prisoners and himself.

Yet Colonel Gooner could never be described as a typical Army officer. He was a man of progressive political views and championed the rights of the indigenous people in a book about his time in India, published after he had left the services. I had always known him as a jolly, amiable old buffer, far removed, one must add, from those many retired Indian Army officers whose brains have perhaps been affected by the heat and dust of the sub-continent. Perhaps readers have come across these poor chaps themselves, the ones who spend their days writing obscure tracts on the Egyptian Pyramids in the reading rooms of public libraries, or travelling to meetings to propound some fanciful idea about a secret international conspiracy of one-legged freemasons or about the Welsh race being descended from one of the lost ten tribes of ancient Israel.

'Where are you off to, my boy?' enquired the Colonel genially.

'I have a luncheon appointment with a friend who I am meeting near Piccadilly Circus,' I said, a statement which, if not false, was certainly economical with the truth as I doubted whether Colonel Gooner would approve of the raffish Jim Jam Club.

'Climb aboard then, I'm going that way myself and it's no trouble whatsoever to drop you off wherever you want,' he said, and not wishing to offend, I complied with his instruction. The Colonel disliked the motor car and owned one of the few horse-driven carriages still to be seen around the West End of London. We lurched forward and then as I sank back against the soft, comfortable seat, one of the horses broke wind with a quite astonishing ferocity.

'Oh, pardon me,' said the Colonel, and though I should have contained myself, I replied, 'That's quite all right, sir. If you hadn't spoken I would have assumed it was the horse.'

But all was well for Colonel Gooner laughed loudly and said, 'Good one, old boy, very good indeed! I must remember to recount your witty riposte at my Club. So how have you been spending your time off in old London town? Enjoying yourself to the full, I'll be bound, and why not for heaven's sake, you're only young once. Tell me though, you must have heard about this grand reception back home for His Majesty in which your father has been involved. I'll be there myself, as my wife's brother is a local landowner near Boroughbridge and he's also on the organising committee for the royal visit.'

He was most pleased when I told him that I was of course going back home for this important event. 'Excellent! Mrs Gooner and I will look forward to seeing you there. We live in the country ourselves as you know, but so many of my old friends live in London that I must spend a couple of weeks here every so often to keep in touch with them.'

We were clipping our way briskly down Shaftesbury Avenue when I called upon the driver to halt. 'I'll get off here, sir, if I may,' I said, shaking hands with the Colonel, 'and I look forward to seeing you again in York.' Little did I realise just how soon I would see him again – far, far sooner than I could have expected!

I crossed the road and bought a button-hole from an itinerant flower seller. My sixpence was received with the usual blessings upon my head and I made my way up Great Windmill Street to the discreet entrance of the Jim Jam Club. Cripps was on duty and was eager to pick up any racing tips, but alas, I had heard nothing further from old Goldhill and was forced to disappoint the porter, who nevertheless passed to me the name of a horse Sir Harold Brown had given him as a good each-way bet in the two o'clock race at Chepstow that afternoon. 'It's a fast filly called Big Brenda, Mr Mountjoy, and I reckon the odds won't be less than twelve to one. What do you think?' he asked me.

'Well now, Cripps,' I said carefully, 'you must be familiar with the old saying, "He who decides to bet each way/Lives to bet another day!"'

'Sir Harold's gone through a lean patch lately and it's about time he picked a winner, so I'll risk a pound each way on Big Brenda. Will you place the bet with Hymie Applebaum for me?'

I gave Cripps two pound notes and sauntered upstairs to the bar. Although it was almost ten past one, there was no sign of Henry Bascombe-Thomas. I sat down and ordered a whisky and soda from a passing waiter and hoped that my absent-minded chum had not forgotten the appointment which he himself had asked me to keep with him.

In fact my worry was unfounded for I had time only to pour the soda into my Scotch when I looked up to see Henry striding towards me. I stood up and greeted him. 'Hello, stranger, how nice to see you again,' I said warmly as we shook hands.

'A pleasure to see you, Rupert,' he responded, pumping my hand. 'I'm so pleased you were free for luncheon. It's been a long time since we broke bread together. To be exact, it would be a couple of days before I sailed for New York when you, Frank Folkestone and Prince Salman laid on a splendid farewell dinner for me at Romano's. So what's the news with you, Rupert? Neither of us wrote to each other as often as we should have done. But Frank Folkestone did mention in one of his letters that your Uncle Humphrey has provided you with the wherewithal for a year off doing very little indeed except fuck pretty girls, you lucky so-and-so! Or has some clever beauty managed to get you to put a ring on her finger?'

I grinned and replied, 'No, though I've fingered quite a few rings since we last met! Still, whilst it's true that I'm taking a break from my studies, you've been to America, which is something I'd love to do. Have you had a rewarding time, Henry? Have you painted much yourself? And what brings you back to Britain?'

'I'll answer your questions in reverse order,' he said with a smile, as we rose and walked into the dining-room where we were seated at one of the best tables overlooking the busy street below. 'I came back simply because my course with Professor Sidney Cohen ended and there was no further need for me to stay in New York.

'And I do still paint, but only for my own pleasure. I now know and accept my limitations, Rupert, which are – well, those of a talented amateur and not a gifted professional. That's how Professor Cohen delivered his verdict on my work and I wasn't too disappointed because the truth is that it wasn't very different to my tutor's back here in Britain.'

The head waiter came up to us and after we

ordered our meal Henry continued, 'His verdict doesn't mean that I can't be involved in the world of art. I've written some critiques for the New York papers and I'd like to do the same in London. I feel I have something to say after spending a year away. God, it was refreshing to leave that dreadful insular resistance to modern painting which one finds here in England. People have told me that third-rate British pictures are still preferred to the new, exciting paintings shown in Paris, Rome and Madrid. I want to help change this head-in-the-sand attitude.

'What's really exciting though, Rupert, is that Professor Cohen, whose influence is very substantial in the New York art world, generously gave my name to Clive Labovitch, the wealthy owner of a leading gallery on Fifth Avenue who wants to set up an exhibition of the most promising, exciting young artists from all over the world. The Professor suggested that I act as his agent in England when I return to London. After discussing the project with me, Mr Labovitch agreed to the proposal, and has transferred five thousand dollars to a bank account over here to be spent on buying for this event which will be staged in New York next Spring.'

Well, naturally, even before Henry had finished speaking I was wondering whether this information would be of use to the lovely Diana Wigmore. I explained to Henry how my closest girl friend was a talented artist who was living in Paris but who would be coming to Britain shortly. An idea struck me – if I could only persuade Henry to come up to York for the grand Royal reception, he would be able to meet Diana and see some of her pictures there, as she was bringing a selection over from France so that Nancy Carrington could have the opportunity to purchase a painting or two for her father's collection.

The only problem was how to interest Henry enough in Diana's work to travel up North so soon after returning to London. Surprisingly, for he showed little interest in politics except to support the radical Liberals, Henry was a staunch Republican and unlike Nancy Carrington, for instance, had no desire whatsoever to hob-nob with the King, so partying with all the swells would have no appeal for him.

But the promise of a good fuck – now that was another matter! I leaned across the table and told him all about Diana, Nancy and the whole business of my going up to see my folks and attending the reception for the King. I invited him to join Nancy and myself and stay a few days with my family at Albion Towers.

'You really must come up with us,' I urged him. 'My parents would be delighted to see you again and you know how interested my mother is in art. She would so enjoy hearing all your news about any up and coming American artists. And talking of up and coming, old boy, Nancy Carrington is a very attractive young lady who simply adores fucking, as does Diana, who particularly liked taking part in a whoresome foursome. I guarantee that you'd be dipping your brush into a fresh pot of paint every night if you take up my invitation.'

Henry's eyes lit up and he said, 'Gosh, you certainly make the trip sound extremely tempting.

But I really have a tremendous amount of work to do in London and I hadn't planned on spending any time out of town. On the other hand, all work and no play makes Jack a dull boy, eh? When do you plan to go?'

'In just over a couple of weeks time,' I replied promptly. 'The big party is on November 15 so Nancy and I thought we'd go up on the previous day. We hadn't decided exactly when we'd go back, but I might stay a few days and visit my Uncle Humphrey and look up some old friends.'

'And you say that I might get the chance to look up some new ones?' Henry quipped wittily. 'I don't think I can pass up such an opportunity, Rupert, so I'll take up your invitation with grateful thanks. I don't mind telling you that I'm in desperate need of a good fuck. Whilst I can't grumble too much about the availability of willing girls in New York, though they are probably a little more inhibited than in London, I've been forced to live like a monk for the month or so. Both the girls I was fucking in Manhattan were unavailable during the last three weeks of my stay and to make matters worse there were no available women on board ship on my journey home.'

'Poor you,' I sympathised, as I refilled his glass with the excellent Club claret. 'Yet I was given to understand that on Atlantic crossings, except during the winter months, there are always a number of unattached females on board eager for masculine company.'

'Maybe, but I was unlucky enough to be a passenger on a ship which was an exception to the rule. The only consolation was that I struck up a friendship with a girl named Jenny Cameron, the Scottish governess of an American family coming to live in London for six months whilst the *pater familias* travelled around Europe on business.

'Jenny was very happy to be coming home to her native Scotland after working for a year in Washington. She was a bonny Scottish lass of twenty-two whose light freckled skin and long reddish hair set off her well-made young body. Perhaps her best attributes were her large breasts which jutted out proudly like two firm spheres.

'Well, on the fourth evening, I engaged her in conversation after dinner and we talked over a lemon squash in one of the lounges (for she was tee-total and I had already put away a bottle of wine during the evening meal). I gazed longingly at these two beauties as we walked back along the deck to our cabins which happened to be very close to each other. Naturally, she slept in the same first class suite as the two children in her charge. After formally shaking hands and parting company at her cabin door, I wished Jenny good-night and I walked back alone very disconsolately to my own quarters.

'I undressed quickly and as it was rather warm in the cabin I lay on the bed naked as I reached over to thumb my way through a copy of *The Oyster*, a "horn" magazine which Frank Folkestone had posted to me every so often. As I thumbed my way through the magazine, the randy stories soon made my shaft stiffen up and demand to be exercised. I took my rock-hard cock in my hand and slowly rubbed it up and down as I closed my eyes and fantasised about running my hands across Jenny's magnificent breasts, of handling her delicious, ripe titties and then placing my hot, throbbing prick in her cunt . . .

'I was on the very verge of spunking when my reverie was disturbed by a gentle knock on my door. I jumped up and called out, "Who's that?" and my heart began to pound when I heard the soft reply, "It's me, Jenny Cameron. Henry, can I come in for a moment?"

'I slipped on a dressing gown and rushed across to open the door where Jenny stood clad in a blue silk night-robe. "Hello, Henry, I hope I haven't disturbed you," she said with a slightly worried look.

' "Not in the slightest, it's lovely to see you again so soon. Is all well though? Are the children all right?"

' "Oh yes, they're sound asleep and won't wake up till morning, so I thought I might join you in a wee night-cap," she said, and then impishly added as she looked slightly downwards, "but I think you had something else on your mind when I knocked on the door."

'I followed her amused gaze downwards and with horror saw that my still erect truncheon was poking out between the folds of my dressing gown. I was so flustered that I sat down heavily on the side of the bed, my face burning and my cock quickly shrank back into its normal flaccid state.

'But to my overwhelming relief, Jenny had not been offended at all by the unintentional exposure of my stiff cock. Far from it, for the sweet girl giggled, sat down next to me and said in her pleasing Midlothian burr, "Dear oh dear, I didn't mean to upset your poor little cockie. Let's bring the shy fellow out again and have a proper look at him."

' "By all means," I said, opening my robe and she reached out and clasped my shrunken shaft in her fingers. As if by magic, it began to swell up again, rapidly returning to its former length and strength as the lovely lass slowly tossed me off, squeezing and rubbing my prick so deliciously that I was almost ready to spend within seconds.

'Then she let her fist stay still as she murmured, "If I let you fuck me, will you promise not to tell anyone? I've only had two or three romps with the children's tutor since leaving home and I'm feeling even more randy than usual after playing with your nice cock. But I must make sure that Mr and Mrs Barbach give me a reference."

' "I swear I won't tell a soul," I panted, and to back up my word I told her of the oath we take at the Jim Jam Club never to reveal the names of lovers. She listened carefully, then smiled and said gaily, "Very well then, you've convinced me, you smooth-talking rogue!"

'Trembling with excitement, I tore off my robe as the delicious girl pulled her night robe over her head and stood stark naked in front of me. I stood up and she walked the few steps towards me, her firm, uptilted breasts jiggling and her strawberry nipples looking up pertly as our mouths met and I clasped her thrilling young body to me.

'We fell backwards on to the bed and my hands

ran over her hard, engorged nipples and her own hand slid down to clasp my pulsating prick which bucked uncontrollably in her sweet grasp. As we threshed around, writhing in each other's arms, my fingers played around the silky strands of red-gold hair which formed a light veil across her pouting little slit. Jenny was justly proud of her pussey for her thighs were full and proportionally formed and my cock leaped and pranced in her hand as it sought access into her dampening cunney. So it was with great excitement that I scrambled to my knees when Jenny wriggled out of my arms and lay flat on her back with her legs apart. Quivering with anticipation I positioned myself between her thighs and gently lowered myself on top of her soft body and a low moan escaped from my throat as she took hold of my truncheon and guided it firmly between her cunney lips into her juicy, wet quim.

'I thrust my yearning cock inside her cunt and when I was fully embedded by the luscious love channel I stayed quite still for a few moments, revelling in the exquisite sensations afforded by her clinging cunney muscles. Then I started to fuck her slowly, pistoning in until our pubic hairs were entwined and then withdrawing all but the tip of my knob before plunging in again to the limit.

'This rich, deep fucking had the desired effect upon Jenny whose rounded bottom cheeks began to roll around as she arched her back, cleverly working her cunt back and forth against the ramming of my thick, hard prick, until I hoarsely groaned that I could no longer hold back the boiling spunk which was shooting up from my tight ballsack.

'Jenny grabbed my arse cheeks and pulled me forward so that every last fraction of my cock was encased in her cunt and our pubic bones mashed together as she started to move her hips up and down. With her hands still on my bum I matched her movements and now my glistening shaft was sliding in and out of her cunney at an even faster pace. With a cry I exploded into her, showering the walls of her love channel with sticky jism. I ejaculated copiously inside her willing pussey and this brought about her own orgasm: her body stiffened and I rubbed her clitty as her cunney was flooded with fresh rivulets of love juice whilst she shuddered in ecstasy as the force of her orgasm swept through her.

'After we had recovered I fucked her from behind as she stood with her feet on the floor, leaning forward with her arms held straight out, the palms of her hands flat against the sheets and her rounded backside pushed out towards me. I slid my shaft between her chubby buttocks and gloried in the sublime sensation as my cock slewed its way into her dripping cunt doggie-style. As before, young Jenny worked her hips in rhythm with my eager thrusts, letting my shaft sink all the way inside her juicy honeypot which I left there momentarily before easing back to piston forward again through the crevice between her bum cheeks.

'This time Jenny was the first to reach journey's end and she cried out, "Go on, Henry! Keep plunging forward! You're coming, aren't you? I can feel your cock shuddering inside my cunt! A-h-r-e! A-h-r-e!" A huge flow of her love juice soaked my shaft and I gasped, "I'm going to spend, Jenny! Yes, yes, I can't hold back any longer!" and I made one last lunge forward, my balls cracking against her bottom as I sent a stream of hot spunk hurtling into her sopping snatch as we collapsed down together on the bed. I'm not sure I could have obliged Jenny with a third bout but fortunately I did not have to try as she looked at my watch and decided she had better go back to her own bed in case one of the children woke up.

'However, after breakfast we exchanged addresses so after staying with you in Yorkshire I might journey on up to Edinburgh as she will be on holiday in mid-November, visiting her parents.'

I sipped my coffee and said, 'Well now, Henry, has the telling of that lascivious anecdote drained you or is your cock still available if required? Since you left our shores for the New World, certain ladies of quality, such as the wives of Army officers serving abroad, have taken to holding discreet little afternoon parties. Entry to these gatherings is not open to all and sundry, however, and to ensure privacy, the ladies leave the names of those members they wish to invite with Cripps and his underlings who pass them on verbally to the lucky chaps chosen to enjoy a wild afternoon's fucking.'

'It looks as though we may be in luck,' commented Henry. 'Look, Cripps has just walked into the restaurant and it looks as though he's coming our way.'

The head porter did indeed make his way to our table but though his message was of good cheer, it was not the news Henry wanted! 'Hope I'm not interrupting you, Mr Mountjoy, but I thought you might like to know that Big Brenda came in second. She was only beaten by a short head but at least you win two pounds.'

'Is that all? I thought you said the horse would be a twelve to one shot,' I said rather disappointedly.

'So it was, sir,' the Club head porter explained patiently, 'but you only get a quarter of the odds for the place and so you win three pounds, but as you lose one of the two pounds of the each-way bet, I'm afraid that you only win a couple of quid. Still, that's better than poor old Sir Harold Brown has done: he had fifty pounds to win on Big Brenda and only had ten pounds each way as a saver.' [British bookmakers are even less generous these days, only offering one fifth of the odds on most each-way bets unless there are more than sixteen runners in the race – Editor]

'Oh well, it's still always better to come out on top,' I said with a sigh, as Cripps handed me my winnings. The crafty porter always made sure that all members' winning bets were paid out with lots of coins which almost always ensured a generous gratuity. As it was Cripps himself who had given me the tip for Big Brenda, I gave him three half-crowns [forty-two and a half pence! – Editor] which naturally put a large smile on his face.

'No afternoon parties today, then?' I enquired or him. He shook his head. 'Not as far as I know, sir,' he replied. 'Though I understand that General Gooner is having a private party with a couple of girls from Swan and Edgar's ladies' underwear department in room nine on the third floor. But please don't say I told you about it, sir.'

I waited till Cripps had left us and then I said to Henry, 'My God! Did you hear that? I never knew General Gooner was a member of the Jim Jam.' And I told Henry how the General had seen me before lunch and had given me a lift in his carriage. I laughed and said, 'To think I fibbed and said I was meeting a friend nearby because I was worried that the old boy might know about this place and would report my coming here to my father! Come on, my dear chap, let's go upstairs and see if the General is still firing his artillery.'

Before we went upstairs Henry insisted on signing the bill for our meal and urged me to hurry as I said that I first wished to visit the cloakroom. When we finally reached the door of room nine, to no great surprise, we found it was locked. 'Damn and blast!' cursed Henry, but I put a restraining hand on his arm and withdrew a silver key from my jacket pocket.

'Do you remember when Count Gewirtz of Galicia paid for the Club to be totally redecorated about five years ago?' I said, grinning at the look of frustration on Henry's face. 'Well, mixed in with the altruistic motive behind the Count's generous gesture was the rather darker desire to own a set of skeleton keys to the private rooms and he paid for a secret set to be made for him. These keys weren't simply used to embarrass other people, although you know how the Count enjoys a good practical joke and one afternoon he used his key to burst in to a room dressed as a policeman just as Lady Pachnos was about to sit upon Mr George Bernard Shaw's quivering naked stiffstander.

'But what the Count actually wanted was to be able to nip into a room without even having to book it with the staff, so nobody, but nobody knew he was there. This facility was not really necessary as far as he was concerned, but it was of great importance for high-ranking personages. They even say his friend Mr Tum Tum [London Society's nickname for the portly King Edward VII – Editor] has used this facility to bring Mrs Keppel and Mrs Quentonne here for a quick fuck.

'However, be that as it may, Cripps somehow found out about the Count's little game and bribed a locksmith to make him a similar set of keys and he sells copies of them at a vast profit to selected Club members.

'Frankly, I wasn't in the market for such items but I happen to have the key to the third floor rooms as I won it from Tubby Meredith at a baccarat evening a few months ago. Now so long as the General hasn't bolted the door, I don't think we'll have too much trouble in joining his little party.'

Henry was very impressed and he rubbed his hands in glee. 'Here's hoping,' he said, as I turned the key and gently pushed against the door which yielded to my weight. 'Hey presto,' I said softly, as I slowly opened it and we popped our heads round to see exactly what military manoeuvre was being attempted by General Gooner, whose heavy breathing we could hear before we saw for ourselves what was taking place.

Well, whilst I did not expect to see the General standing in front of a blackboard, lecturing on lessons to be learned from the Boer War, I was still taken aback at the sight which greeted our eyes. For there on the bed, stark naked and flat on his back the gallant veteran lay with his hands clasped behind his neck. His chest was covered with matted grey hair and without the restrictions imposed by a belt, his corpulent belly sagged all over the place. But his gnarled old penis was standing up smartly enough, a thick, twitching love truncheon which was being manipulated by the buxom Maisie, one of the Jim Jam's barmaids, who was dressed, or more accurately half-undressed, in her black Club uniform. She was kneeling on the bed beside him and was still wearing her skirt but, in all probability assisted by General Gooner, she had taken off her blouse and chemise and her large, bare breasts looked mouth-wateringly ripe for a touch of masculine lips or fingers.

We stood silently at the door, watching with growing interest as Maisie squealed, 'Stanley, please undo the buttons of my skirt so I can take it off before you fuck me.'

'Certainly, my dear, I'll do my level best but I don't know whether my old John Thomas is up to much today,' said the General doubtfully. However, he helped unbutton Maisie's skirt and she stopped frigging his prick in order to peel off her knickers and stockings. When she was naked she took hold of his cock in both hands but I could see that his tool had now wilted and despite some vigorous frigging and tonguing, Maisie seemed unable to coax it back up to an erection.

'Maybe this will help your old soldier stand to attention,' Maisie suggested, as she knelt in front of him, facing the curtained bay window. She stuck out her sumptuous backside and the General placed his hands on her rich, rounded bum cheeks and parted them to give himself a close-up view of her hairy pussey pouch and her wrinkled little bum-hole, whilst at the door Henry and I were also treated to a tantalising glimpse of the fur lined lips of her cunt.

Maisie raised her buttocks and the General spread them open even further, showing her to be wet and open and she turned her head towards him and said, 'I'm ready and waiting for inspection, sir.' But he shook his head and looked sadly down at his flaccid shaft which flapped feebly against his thigh. 'Sorry, m'dear, it looks as though I shall be forced to run up the white flag even before battle commences. Gad, if I were only ten years younger, I would have had a massive boner by now! But lately, my treacherous old plonker has been playing the most diabolical games with me.

'Strange to think that when I was a young lad I had only to think fleetingly of a juicy cunt and it would swell up in an instant. All the working girls who serviced the cadets at Sandhurst used to say that Stanley Gooner's cock was the thickest and hardest of them all,' he added gloomily. 'Nowadays though, merely striving for a stiffie is enough to put paid to all hope of my achieving one.'

'Never mind, dear,' said Maisie comfortingly. 'I'll tell you what, why don't I lie down and you can bring me off with your fingers instead?'

She settled herself down next to him and began to squeeze her own engorged nipples. 'Now then, Stanley, rub my clitty, there's a good boy,' she ordered, as she continued to massage her horned up teats. 'Ah, that's very nice, and slide your fingers in my cunney whenever you like, I'm getting really moist. Mmm, keep going, you'll have me going off in no time at all.'

The General turned to the side and their mouths met in a passionate kiss. Then he bent his head down and while Maisie rolled one rubbery nipple between her thumb and forefinger, he sucked deeply on the other tawny tittie. Soon he was sliding three fingers up to the hilt inside her sopping slit and she threshed around wildly, her feet drumming a tattoo on the sheets as she tried to work herself off.

Alas, it was obvious to Henry and I that she was having as little success as her partner, whose penis still lay obstinately limp despite all the action around it. 'Don't you think we should help out?' muttered Henry, who had already taken off his jacket and was unbuckling his belt.

'Oh yes, most certainly we should,' I said with a grin as I loosened my cravat. 'I would even go so far as to say that it is our bounden duty as Jim Jammers [as Club members were known – Editor] to aid Maisie reach her climax.'

It took only a few short moments before we too were as naked as babes and we padded briskly up to the bed, our two stiff cocks standing almost up against our bellies. Our footsteps were heard by Maisie who sat up and gaped at us. 'What the hell—'

'It's the cavalry, Maisie, arriving just in time to ensure you enjoy a good spend! Seriously, don't worry, it's only me, Rupert Mountjoy and Henry Bascombe-Thomas. He's a Club member too but he's been away for some time so you might not recognise him.'

She grinned lewdly at us. 'Who says I don't? His face has changed especially now he's shaved off his moustache, but I'd recognise Henry's roundheaded cock anywhere.'

I looked down at Henry's bulging boner and sure enough, Maisie's memory was absolutely spot-on, for like the handful of Jewish boys at St Lionel's and my close chum Prince Salman, who was a Mohammedan, Henry's slightly curved pecker was bereft of its foreskin.

'I'm truly honoured that you remember the shape of my tadger, Maisie,' said Henry politely. 'Though I'm damned if I can think where on earth you might have seen it before.'

'Dear, oh dear, still the absent professor, aren't you? Just before you went away – to America, if I'm not mistaken – the Club committee gave you a farewell supper followed by a presentation by one of the girls from Mrs Wickley's place in Macclesfield Street. I can't believe you'd forget *that*!'

Henry gave a loud chuckle as he stroked his throbbing tool. 'No, of course not – who could forget such a grand send-off! I thought the girl was going to present me with a wallet, a picture-frame or some momento of the Club. Much to my delight, she presented me with her pussey and I seem to recall that I fucked her on the dining-room table in the Harcourt Suite.'

'Quite right, and I was serving behind the bar and happened to notice how the knob of your love trunk had been bared, presumably when it was only a tiny sapling!'

'How observant of you! Yes, my parents took the advice of the learned Doctor Aigin of Harley Street who recommended the operation when as a very small boy I had an irritating rash on the skin round my helmet. I hardly remember the operation – which perhaps is just as well!'

At this point General Gooner, who had understandably been very quiet during these exchanges, snorted loudly and thundered, 'Come now, gentlemen, enough of this idle chatter. For heaven's sake do your duty and fuck this poor girl without further delay. God knows she's been kept waiting long enough for a thick, stiff prick of whatever shape or size.'

'Thank you, Stanley,' she said with a giggle. She took each of our two rampant rods in her soft hands and began to frig our stiff shafts. 'Well now boys, I can hardly fuck you both together, so who's going to be the first to cram his cock inside my juicy cunney?'

'After you, Henry,' I said generously. 'You were bemoaning the fact that your prick hasn't seen too much action lately.'

'That's dashed kind of you, Rupert,' he said with gratitude, as General Gooner heaved himself up to sit on a nearby easy chair and Maisie lay back and opened her legs, exposing her damp pussey to Henry. Without further ado he crawled between her spread thighs and immediately parted her serrated cunney lips with the tip of his cock.

'Go on, shove it right up as far as you can,' she panted, and, nothing loath, he rammed his veiny pole deep inside her clinging cunney. The General and I watched Henry's gleaming cock slide its squelchy path in and out until Maisie whispered a few words to Henry who grinned – and without missing a stroke, rolled over so that he was now on his back and Maisie was sitting astride him. She pivoted happily on his shaft, rhythmically rocking to and fro as he thrust upwards, plunging his pulsing prick up inside her warm wetness. His back arched upwards as Maisie worked her soft, moist flesh against his iron-hard staff and as they spent simultaneously their surging cries of fulfilment echoing around the room as her cunt milked the manly essence out of his shuddering penis until he withdrew his sated, shrinking shaft from her love channel.

The happy pair lay panting with the effort of their joust but General Gooner cleared his throat and broke the silence. 'Now then, don't just stand there like a lemon, young Mountjoy, what the deuce are you waiting for?' he cried, like a demented sergeant-major. 'You young fellows don't seem to know you're born! Isn't it obvious that Maisie needs a second seeing-to? Damn it all, when I was your age I would have been up and at her as soon as you could say Jack Robinson.'

'I am right, aren't I, m'dear?' he asked Maisie,

who reached out and pulled my twitching tool towards her as she replied, 'Well, I wouldn't say no, that's for sure, especially with such a nice-looking young cock ready and waiting to ream out my tingling pussey.'

I climbed onto the bed next to Henry with Maisie still clutching my cock. She leaned forward and brought her lips to my knob, rolling her tongue around the purple dome and giving me playful little nips with her pearly white teeth. My prick began to pulse furiously in her mouth as she greedily gobbled my throbbing tool and her eyes smouldered with passion as I sat up and cupped her full breasts with my hands, deftly flicking her nipples with my nails.

She now began to give me sharp little licks on my swollen shaft, followed by a series of quick kisses up and down the stem, encompassing my hairy ballsack and she ran her lips down to my perineum, the so-sensitive zone between the balls and arse-hole, which sent waves of pleasure floating through my body. Then she thrust my cock in and out of her mouth, deep into her throat and she tongued me at the end of every stroke, lapping up the pearly of creamy white fluid which was already beginning to seep out of the 'eye' on the tip of my helmet.

My arse began to undulate as she grasped the base of my shaft and sucked hard on my bulbous knob, but as soon as she felt I was on the verge of spending, she made ready to swallow my spunk. I thrust my hips upwards and my cock shuddered violently between her lips as with a long spasm I released my sperm, first in a few early shoots and then in crashing dollops of frothy hot jism which filled her mouth and oozed out from between her lips. Maisie let the sticky white love juice flow down her throat as she gently teased my spongy knob with her tongue as very gradually I allowed the wet shaft to slide free.

I thought that this little orgy would now end but General Gooner was standing up, holding his now rampant cock as he cried out happily, 'Well done, Maisie, that was a splendid sucking off. Just watching you at work has finally done the trick and given me a cockstand.'

'Quick, come over here and fuck me,' she laughed. 'I had a good little spend whilst I was sucking Rupert's prick so my cunney's wet and waiting for your thick, fat shaft.'

'Strike whilst the iron's hot, eh?' he grunted, as he clambered on top of her and Henry and I scrambled up and stood by the side of the bed, watching the game old boy mount Maisie and guide home his ramrod between her yielding cunney lips.

Once he was fully embedded in her, Maisie trapped his cock inside her cunt by lacing her feet together behind his back. The General could hardly pump in and out of her pussey because her cunney muscles were gripping him so tightly, so instead he slid his hand under her and inserted the tip of his forefinger inside her bum-hole which sent such powerful sensations running through her that she squealed and wriggled in an ecstasy of passion. This also made her shift her legs and the General was now able to piston in and out, fucking at a surprisingly high speed, bringing Maisie off time and again as the fierce momentum sent fresh thrilling spasms of pleasure out from her drenched pussey.

Maisie knew that it would be unfair to ask the General to over-exert himself and so she brought her legs up against the small of his broad back, humping the lower half of her body upwards to meet the violent strokes of his raging rod. But as he bore down on her yet again, she grabbed his balls in her hand and tenderly squeezed their hairy sack. This had the desired effect of hastening his spend and seconds later his body tensed and with a hoarse cry of 'Steady the Buffs!' he crashed down upon her, his cock jetting its jism inside her sopping slit as she clenched her thighs together until she had extracted every last drain of cream from his spurting shaft.

I applauded the General on his prowess as a veteran cocksman. 'Well done, sir, I'm sure neither Henry nor myself could have bettered you for technique,' I said with total sincerity, although the gallant old soldier would accept no praise and waved aside my congratulations.

'Thank 'ee, my boy, but you should have seen me in my prime. Then I could have brought Maisie to the boil, cooled her down, and brought her up again at least five times before shooting my load. But gone are those roistering years back with the regiment when I could fuck all night with the lovely Gita, the beautiful dark-skinned daughter of the Maharajah of Bangitin, who was a true expert in eastern erotic arts, and then take part in the special short-arm parade of the officers of Ninth Punjabi Rifles organised by our

Colonel's lady wife, whose favourite breakfast consisted of mouthfuls of fresh spunk obtained by sucking off the cocks of her three favourite young subalterns, Brandon Smith, Charles Farnes-Barnes and myself.'

'How very interesting, General,' said Henry with a puzzled look. 'My uncle Eric was for many years Governor of Bangitin and he never mentioned the Ninth Punjabis to me, nor is there any mention of them in his memoirs.'

Oh-ho, I thought, so the old goat might be guilty of embroidering his tale. But at St Lionel's, it was firmly dinned into the pupils that it is the height of bad manners to question the accuracy of another gentleman's story, especially if it were entertaining, so I held my peace. Nevertheless, I filed the incident away in my memory in the unlikely event of ever having to persuade General Gooner not to tell my father about my escapades at the Jim Jam Club – but as he could hardly do this without seriously compromising himself, I was not unduly concerned about details of my secret life finding their way to the ears of my parents!

General Gooner himself confirmed this belief whilst we helped ourselves liberally to the sandwiches, fresh fruits and chilled white wine which he had ordered to be on hand before (as he had mistakenly thought) he had locked himself and Maisie away from any prying eyes!

'Er, gentlemen, I don't think there is any need to mention details of this afternoon's activities to a living soul,' he said, tapping his fingers nervously on the arm of his chair. 'Don't you agree that the three of us promise to keep silent about our fun and games – for Maisie's sake, if nothing else.'

'Yes, of course,' I said gravely, giving Henry a broad wink. 'I'm sure that none of us would want to compromise her reputation as one of the Club's most valued employees.'

'Good, that's settled then,' said the General with obvious relief. 'I'm truly glad you chaps happened to be passing and helped the party go with a swing, though I'm still puzzled as to why you wanted to come into room nine this afternoon, let alone how you managed to open the door, for I would have sworn on a stack of bibles that I had locked it after Maisie and I slipped upstairs after luncheon.'

'Maybe you turned the key the wrong way, sir,' said Henry disingenuously. 'I've done that myself occasionally. But the reason why we came in here was that we understood that Lord Searle had booked the room for a showing of the new naughty films he brought back from Paris last week.'

'Oh, that's not till six o'clock,' said Maisie, who probably knew full well that one of us had purchased one of Cripps' skeleton keys, but who had enjoyed the afternoon's sport and was more than satisfied with General Gooner's little present of five pounds for her participation. 'You must have misread the notice pinned up on the Forthcoming Attractions board.'

I offered our apologies for this mistake but, as the General said, everything turned out for the best so we parted friends.

As we went downstairs, I suggested a game of snooker but Henry looked at his watch and said regretfully that he must be going as his Aunt Clare was expecting him to take tea with her. We shook hands and he said, 'Rupert, I so enjoyed seeing you again. Will you confirm all the arrangements for our trip up to York? I'm staying at the Club until I find a decent apartment, so if need be you can always leave a message with Cripps.'

After he took his leave I went into the writing-room and dashed off a letter to my parents. I told them that I had bumped into General Gooner in Bedford Square (though I omitted to mention the later meeting!) and that in addition to Nancy Carrington, I had now invited Henry Bascombe-Thomas to stay with us and hoped that this would not be an inconvenience. I added that if an invitation to the party could be wangled for Henry, so much the better, but this was not of prime importance for the main purpose of his visit was to assess the worth of Diana Wigmore's pictures.

I handed the letter in to the desk to be posted and went back into the lounge for a snooze. As I dozed off, the thought passed through my mind that whilst I have never suffered from insomnia, the noted Society physician, Doctor Aigin of Harley Street, has always maintained that fucking is by far the best cure in the world for this troublesome complaint. I would go further and add that the activity is efficacious for many other complaints as well, except perhaps for the common cold, a cure for which has so far eluded the medical profession. However, in my experience, a small whisky to soothe the throat followed by a rattling good fuck will at least temporarily banish the miseries of a feverish chill.

CHAPTER THREE

Art for Art's Sake

FOR THE SAKE OF BREVITY I will mention only briefly the events which took place between my reunion with Henry Bascombe-Thomas at the Jim Jam Club and the brisk November morning just over a fortnight later when Henry met Nancy Carrington and myself at King's Cross Station for our journey up to Albion Towers, our family's estate, which lies on the edge of the Forest of Knaresborough, some six miles or so outside Harrogate.

By a supreme effort of will, I fucked Mary the maid just one more time during this period, to be precise, on the evening of my departure to Yorkshire, and that was at her insistence. I, perhaps foolishly, asked her what she would like as a small present for taking on, so cheerfully, many extra duties when my housekeeper, Mrs Harrow, was laid low with a nasty bout of influenza.

Otherwise, I had no further erotic adventures of note, except of course those which took place during the wild evening enjoyed with Nancy Carrington which I had arranged, as mentioned earlier in this narrative, when I reciprocated her invitation for the wonderful luncheon party and the splendid orgy with Countess Marussia of Samarkand. Nancy came over to dine with myself and my cousin, Michael Reynolds, a lusty young medical student though unfortunately his current *amour*, the pretty little Shella de Souza who I also earlier mentioned *en passant*, was at the last minute prevented from joining us by the onset of the same indisposition which had affected Mrs Harrow.

However, Lady Knuckleberry, my next door neighbour, returned to town that very afternoon from a few days at Sir Michael Bailey's country house in West Sussex, and very kindly agreed to make up the numbers at my dinner party. Furthermore, she turned out to be a willing participant when later in the evening Nancy suggested a game of 'Blind Man's Cock' in which Edwards and Mary were also invited to take part, and she thoroughly enjoyed her reward of being fucked by both Michael Reynolds and Edwards as I tongued Nancy's hairy cunt whilst Mary sucked my rampant prick.

Naturally, on the day of our journey up North, Nancy accepted my offer of transport to King's Cross and so as not to risk being late because of an absence of taxis, I ordered a Prestoncrest chauffeur and motor car for the short journey to the station. We were in good time to meet Henry who had already arrived from his new apartment in Philimore Gardens, Kensington. I introduced my old friend to Nancy Carrington, saying that I hoped they would both wish to buy Diana

Wigmore's works and bid against each other in auction. I spoke only half in jest as Diana did need a substantial sum to continue living in France because her parents wanted her to come home and meet more suitable young men than she was mixing with on the Left Bank in Paris.

Whilst our luggage was being loaded onto the train, I was curious to see Henry walk over to the station bookstall and whisper a few words as he passed over some coins to a sales assistant, who then reached down under the counter and gave Henry a large sealed brown envelope in which I assumed was a magazine which he slipped under his arm. I said nothing at the time but as soon as we were settled in our first-class compartment – and to our great satisfaction we were not burdened by the company of other passengers – I asked Henry what publication he had bought at King's Cross to read on the journey.

'Oh, just something light to while away the time,' he said carelessly, as, spot on time, the locomotive pulling our train hissed loudly and began to slowly chug its way out of the station. Henry did not further enlighten me as to the nature of his purchase but neatly changed the subject saying, 'I've brought some writing paper with me if either of you wish to catch up on any correspondence. After all, even though this service runs non-stop to Leeds, we still have nearly three hours to kill until we change trains there.'

'Thank you, but I can think of better things to do in a railway carriage, Mr Bascombe-Thomas,' said Nancy saucily, putting her hand on Henry's knee.

I queried her statement and asked, 'Better things to do? Such as what?'

'Fucking, of course, you silly boy,' she said brightly. 'Especially during the day, I don't think that a railway carriage can be beaten when it comes to finding a suitable place to indulge oneself.'

Henry looked at her blankly at first and then his lips broadened out slowly into a lascivious smile. 'Really, Miss Carrington? I don't think I have ever had the pleasure of testing your interesting hypothesis although I can well imagine the excitement of bucking one's hips in rhythm with the clickity clack of the wheels passing over the rails. Yes, the words of Thomas Grey come to mind, "No speed with this, can fleetest horse compare,/No weight like this, canal or Vessel bear."

'And I recall reading a thrilling little tale in *The Oys*—, ah, a magazine to which I subscribe, about a young couple making love on the London-Manchester express. The boy came at Crewe, the girl climaxed at Stoke and they both spent together at Rugby and Watford.'

'They were fortunate not to have been interrupted,' I commented. Henry nodded his head. 'They were fortunate indeed,' he agreed with a smile. 'But the ticket collector was a good sport and a sovereign bought his compliance to wait until the train was approaching Euston before inspecting their tickets and the ripe, nubile nakedness of the girl concerned.'

'Have you ever fucked a nice juicy pussey on a train, Rupert?' asked Nancy, and I was forced to admit that this was a pleasure I had yet to experience. But I added, 'Mind you, I'll never forget a fine time I had on a train with a randy girl when I was in my last term at St Lionel's.'

'Did you, Rupert?' said Henry, raising his eyebrows. 'I don't recall your ever mentioning it to me.'

'I didn't tell anybody, not even Frank Folkestone who had shared my study for the previous two years. You see, the girl concerned was the daughter of an employee of the school and I was concerned about her reputation as well as the fact that if news of the incident had reached the bursar's ears, he might have dismissed her father.'

Nancy's eyes shone with emotion as she moved up closer to me on the seat and said, 'That did you great credit, Rupert, and shows that even in your youth you acted like a true English gentleman. However, four years have now passed and perhaps now you feel able to reveal exactly what occurred.'

I thought for a moment and then said, 'Yes, I see no reason why I should keep the secret any longer.

'It happened when the First Eleven went to Winchester to play cricket. Normally, I would never have been in the side for I am no great lover of the game and have never been more than average with either bat or ball. But a couple of chaps had to cry off for one reason or another and I found myself included as twelfth man. I could have declined the invitation but being the reserve was no hardship as I didn't really want a game and on a fine day there are many worse things to do than watch your friends running around from the comfort of a deckchair with a glass of iced lemonade in one hand and a good book in the other.

'Well, one of my few duties consisted of bringing on a tray of cold drinks to the team during a short break in play whilst we were out in the field. I managed to perform this hardly onerous chore but walking back briskly to the pavilion, I caught my right foot in a small pothole and severely wrenched it. I was in great pain and at first it was thought I might have broken a bone. However, although the foot ballooned out, the pain slowly subsided, but the Winchester matron advised me to keep my foot from the ground for as long as possible.

'The match ended quite early as for some reason St Lionel's has never had a good cricket side since the old days of James St John thirty years ago. We were skittled out for only eighty-three runs and Mr Dexter, the master in charge of our party, decided that the team could catch the five forty-five train back to Chichester. "It might be a good idea for you to stay and take a later train, Mountjoy," he suggested, and the Winchester chaps made me most welcome, carrying me into the sixth form common-room and standing me a slap-up high tea.

'By seven o'clock, the swelling on my foot was going down and the bruise was beginning to come out. As it was unlikely that I had inflicted any lasting damage, I decided to ask for a lift to the station and catch the seven twenty train. Mr

Dexter had left me some cash with a train ticket so in the unlikely event of there being no taxis at Chichester, I could always telephone the school and ask for a cart to be sent for me.

'I was given a walking stick and driven to Winchester station in the school porter's pony and trap and I managed to hobble on to the train without too much difficulty. The carriage was empty except for a girl whose pretty face I vaguely recognised sitting in the "ladies only" compartment of the carriage [recently there has been talk of reintroducing these compartments for the comfort of modern female travellers – Editor] reading a newspaper and I placed myself out of her field of vision as one of the Winchester chaps had passed me a copy of *Cremorne Gardens* and I was dying to read this horny book.'

I turned my head to look at Nancy, who was now snuggled up beside me with her hand on my thigh, and continued, 'No-one else entered the carriage at Winchester nor at the first few stations. Then the train slowed to a halt in the middle of nowhere and the guard came through to tell us that we would be delayed twenty minutes because of a buckled rail further down the line. Well, this was the ideal opportunity to take out my book and I avidly read the saucy tale about the randy romps of Penny and Katie, the two pretty daughters of Sir Paul and Lady Arkley.

'Their naughty escapades with the gardener's boy soon made my prick swell up though I made no effort to hide the bulge in my lap which pushed hard against the material of my flannels. Idly, my fingers strayed down to caress my cock

150

but I was rudely shaken out of my erotic reverie by the sound of a muffled girlish giggle. I looked up and to my horror saw that the girl I had seen sitting in the far corner of the carriage had, unnoticed by me, moved out of her compartment and moved into mine via the corridor.

'As you may well imagine, I gasped with embarrassment and my cheeks flamed bright red as I crossed my legs in a vain attempt to hide my tumescent crotch. Then I foolishly tried to blurt out an apology but I struggled hard to find the right words. After all, I could hardly say, "Please pardon my prick," and just continue reading as if nothing had happened. But as it turned out I was in luck, for the attractive young miss burst out laughing and said, "Please don't apologise, for that's not the first time I've seen a man with his shaft straining to be freed from his trousers. Anyway, it was rude of me to disturb you when you were so engrossed in your book. May I see what you were reading? I'm sure that it must be a jollier read than the newspaper I bought at Winchester Station."

'She stretched out her hand to take the book in question which I was weakly holding over my cock which was still sticking up in my lap. "Gosh, this really is hot stuff!" she said, as she flicked through the pages. "Where did you get it from, Rupert? I suppose you'll give it to Frank Folkestone or Prince Salman when you've finished it because I'll bet that *Cremorne Gardens* can't be found in the library at St Lionel's! However, you never know, perhaps Dr Keeleigh keeps his own private copy under lock and key in the headmaster's study, away from the prying eyes of his scholars."

' "I somehow doubt it," I replied, now feeling more at ease despite being quite perplexed by her knowledge of my name and of my school. "But you seem to know a great deal about me, even though we've never met. And I'm certain we haven't met, by the way, as I would certainly have remembered such a pretty face as yours if I had ever been honoured by the pleasure of an introduction to you."

'She brushed back a lock of golden blonde hair which had fallen over her face and two charming dimples appeared at the corners of her mouth as she smiled and said, "Thank you for the compliment, kind sir. Well, it's true that we haven't exactly been formally introduced but surely you must have noticed me walking around the school playing fields whilst you were practising at the nets."

' "The playing fields?" I repeated, for I was puzzled by her remark. "No, I can't say that I have ever seen you there, but then I'm not a frequent visitor there as frankly, I'm not all that keen on games. If you are to be found walking nearby, though, I'll change my ways immediately and go to cricket practice every evening. But in return do please tell me how you seem to know all about me."

'This made her laugh and she said, "You are such a smooth talker, Rupert Mountjoy! Well, I'll give you a big clue which should solve the mystery for you. My name is Pauline Hollingsworth. There now, doesn't that information help everything fall into place for you?"

' "Hollingsworth, did you say?" I ruminated and then the penny dropped. "Oh, then you must be one of old Mr Hollingsworth's daughters."

'She clapped her hands to applaud my deduction. "Absolutely right, Rupert, my father, old Mr Hollingsworth as you call him, has been the head groundsman at St Lionel's for the past twelve years and my mother is one of the school cooks. My sisters and I grew up here but now we've all left home. My two sisters are in service near Brighton at Lord and Lady Newman's and I won a scholarship to study at the Chelsea School of Art in London. But I do come back to St Lionel's occasionally and I've heard an awful lot about you and your friends from my friend Melanie the laundrymaid." [See *The Intimate Memoirs Of An Edwardian Dandy Volume One: Youthful Scandals* – Editor]

'I had the grace to blush but Pauline stroked my arm and then let her hand fall to my thigh. "Do you know what Melanie and the other servant girls told me about you, Frank Folkestone and Prince Salman? They said that Frank was hung like a horse, Prince Salman's prick had no foreskin and slipped in very easily – but they judged that out of the three of you, Rupert, you were the best fuck, instinctively knowing how to excite a girl with your tongue and fingers as well as your big cock.

' "I'd love to find out for myself whether they were right," she murmured, letting her hand slide across my lap and squeeze my still semi-erect shaft, before beginning to deftly unbutton my flies.

'I could hardly believe my ears and my whole body began to shake with barely suppressed excitement. I tried to speak but the words just refused to come out as Pauline moved her head closer to mine and whispered, "Now then, Rupert Mountjoy, let me look at the evidence for myself," as she now unbuckled my belt and I lifted my bottom off the seat to allow Pauline to pull down my white flannels. She plunged her fingers inside my undershorts and I let out a little gasp as her warm, soft hand grasped my now rigid tadger and I raised my hips a second time to let my drawers join my trousers around my ankles and to leave my cock and balls in a proud state of nudity.

'Just then there was a loud whistle from the engine, the train lurched forward and we slowly began to move along through the thankfully deserted countryside. "Blast, there won't be time for a fuck but that looks like a splendid meaty cock – and what a large ballsack you have for a boy of your age. Oh, Rupert, I must draw out some spunk and see how spicy your spunk tastes!" I looked at her glassily, not believing I could have heard her uninhibited remark correctly, but without further ado she took a firm grip around my pulsating prick and bending down, swirled her tongue around my bulbous purple knob. She sucked lustily, noisily gobbling upon my throbbing tool which twitched and bucked in her mouth as her moist pink tongue travelled up and down the length of my pulsing shaft.

'This delicious stimulation soon brought me to the brink of a spend and then with an immense shudder, my creamy emission gushed out of my cock and flowed down her throat. Pauline skilfully sucked up the last drops of sperm and then she fell away from me, licking her rich, full lips with evident enjoyment. "Mmm, that was quite delicious," she commented, as she recovered her senses. "Your jism isn't as salty as my boy friend's or that of Dr Brooke, my college lecturer."

' "Your college lecturer?" I said in surprise, as I pulled up my drawers and trousers and began buttoning myself up.

' "All the girls in my class have sucked his prick at one time or another – and none of us ever fails to gain passes on his courses!" she replied, as the train picked up speed and we rattled along towards our destination. Of course, I would have preferred to fuck the sweet girl but as she had rightly remarked, there would not have been adequate time as the driver did his best to make up for the lost time and the only thing worse than a hurried fuck is no fuck at all!

'Anyway, we were only ten minutes late in reaching Chichester and we commandeered a hansom to take us back to St Lionel's. But Pauline only stayed a brief while with her parents before going off again to London and I have never seen her since that glorious afternoon.'

I closed my eyes and sighed as I recalled that blissful journey and my mind had been so filled with the pleasant remembrance of this lively interlude that I had not noticed how my saucy anecdote had affected Nancy, who had raised her skirt, pulled down her knickers and was busy frigging herself by gently rubbing her fingers against the lips of her moistening cunney. Looking back on this scenario, I am certain that it was not only my graphic storytelling which made the lovely lass feel so randy, but also the gentle rocking of the carriage which many ladies have confessed to me makes them highly conducive to voluptuous ideas.

'Let's re-enact Rupert's lascivious story,' suggested Henry, whose stiff cock had formed a Himalayan peak in the elegant new trousers he had picked up from Mr Rabinowitz's workshop only the night before.

'A splendid idea,' Nancy enthused, ceasing her frigging to begin unbuttoning her blouse. 'Rupert, be a dear and lock the door, please.'

I stood up and performed this simple favour whilst my fellow travellers started to tear off their clothes in an ever increasing frenzy. When they were naked, Nancy and Henry moved into a passionate clinch and they fell back upon the seat with Nancy's soft hands smoothing over his slim body, sending my friend into a rapture of sensual delight. Then moving quickly, she scrambled over him and bent her head down to engage his lips in a burning kiss. They moved their thighs together until their pubic muffs rubbed roughly against each other as they now rolled over into the more usual position with Nancy flat on her back and Henry between her parted legs, his slightly tanned body fairly trembling with excitement. I could see Henry's thick, hard shaft throbbing with a powerful intensity as his circumcised cock probed the entrance to her exquisite loveslit and I aided the lewd pair by taking Henry's cock between my fingers and guiding his helmet between Nancy's pouting cunney lips. They cried out their joint thanks as his pulsing boner slid home, massaging her clitty as he embedded his proud prick inside the juicy love channel which so lovingly welcomed it.

Watching this storm of passion sent my own cock sky high and for the sake of comfort I was forced to unbutton my trousers and bring out my swollen shaft which stood stiffly to attention as I watched Henry's prick slew in and out of Nancy's sopping cunt. My trusty right hand flew to my cock and began frigging as Henry arched his back upwards and then crashed down upon Nancy's soft curves. We all came together and the wonderful feeling shuddered through every pore as I pumped spurt after spurt of sticky spunk over the entwined lovers, who were writhing in their own paroxyms of pleasure.

Alas, as I coated the couple with sperm, Henry turned his head towards me and received a great glob of jism in his left eye which brought the proceedings to a somewhat inglorious end and after wiping ourselves down with a towel from my travelling case, we dressed ourselves and I unlocked the door of the compartment.

It was just as well that we did not continue this frenetic frolic, because within only a few minutes an inspector appeared to clip our tickets and to announce that luncheon would shortly be served in the restaurant car. We trooped in to the dining car and I should mention that I was agreeably surprised by the quality of our luncheon which consisted of an excellent clear soup, after which came a generous slice of turbot with anchovy sauce, followed by a main offering of tender duckling with new potatoes and green peas. The dessert of a gooseberry tart and cream was also first class, as was the Stilton cheese with which we concluded the meal. The service was cheerful and attentive and I was impressed with the care which had been taken to ensure that the silver service really sparkled in the sunlight which was surprisingly strong for a late autumnal day. All in all we thought the luncheon very good value even at the relatively high price of four shillings and sixpence. [Only twenty-two and a half pence, which shows how inflation has robbed us of our currency during the twentieth century! – Editor] As I had paid for the bottle of Chardonnay we drank with our food, Henry insisted on paying for our meal and he was thanked effusively for the handsome gratuity by the two waiters.

After coffee, we sauntered back to our compartment and Nancy said to me with genuine regret in her voice, 'I'm dreadfully sorry, Rupert, but would you mind waiting till this evening when perhaps we can make love before dinner? I know how frustrated you must feel after seeing Henry fuck me just now but frankly, I'm feeling so tired after that delicious lunch that I'd rather close my eyes for half an hour or so.'

'Please don't give it another thought,' I replied truthfully. 'I'd also appreciate forty winks and I'm pretty sure that Henry will be pleased to follow suit.'

'I will indeed,' said Henry, taking off his jacket and settling himself down for a nice little nap. 'Wake me up when we get near Leeds.'

In less than five minutes both my companions were fast asleep, worn out too, no doubt, by their brief but intense bout of pre-prandial fucking. Although I was also feeling tired I was not actually sleepy so I decided to read for a while. Then on the seat next to Henry, my eye caught sight of the mysterious brown envelope which had been passed to him at the King's Cross bookstall. The flap was open so I carefully pulled the envelope towards me and took out the magazine which had been stuffed inside. My face crinkled into a broad smile as I saw that Henry had bought a copy of *The Latest Letters and Verses of Jenny Everleigh*. I eagerly thumbed through the pages, as the Everleigh horn books were highly prized both at St Lionel's and at Oxford University where even second-hand copies were sold for as much as two shillings each. [Several volumes of Jenny Everleigh's erotic diaries have recently been republished in paperback form, though most of her correspondence and poetry has been lost – Editor]

It took a minute to two to fully appreciate the following verse:

Come Teddy dear, lay your body down
Upon your lover's naked belly white,
Now raptures soon shall our embraces crown;
This is the path to sheer delight.

I know the lessons I have learned from you,
Sweet teachings in the flowery path of love,
Sure I'll remember all I must do,
When I am under and you are above!
Each day upon my cunt your burning kisses fall,
Each movement of your tongue gives me such bliss,
Till no longer for your cock I can forbear to call!

And at this point I rumbled that this poem was a clever if rude acrostic and possibly written – as Jenny had certainly been fucked by His Gracious Majesty King Edward VII during his wild years as Prince of Wales – for the King. My suspicions were confirmed on the very next page on which was printed a love letter from Jenny to A – E –, surely Prince Albert Edward himself. As we were soon to meet the great man, I read this epistle to him with especial interest . . .

My Dearest,

If your duties allow you, come round to my Aunt Portia's house, number sixty-nine, Exhibition Road (a felicitous address in the circumstances, don't you think?) around midday on Thursday and I'll suck your noble prick whilst you are bringing me off with your tongue and then you'll fuck me with your big cock all afternoon!

How I missed you last night at the soirée Lady Linda Brighton gave for Signor Marchiano, the new Italian ambassador. Not only was I bored but I had to fend off the unwanted attentions of Sir Oswald Holland and his friend Colonel Grahame – even the amusing charms of Dr Jonathan Letchmore who rescued me from the randy pair could not fill the void in my heart.

What would I give to have your hands freely roaming

across my nude body as they did that night after Lord Zane's ball! But I shall have to make do with my imagination and the beautiful dildo made by Monsieur Tihanyi, fashioned upon your own royal measurements. I am sitting on my bed quite naked and I am looking in the mirror at the silky blonde pussey hair which curls around my crack. Now I am moving my hands slowly across my breasts, cupping the firm globes and rolling my palms over the upright red stalky nipples which have risen up to greet them.

Darling, I am whispering your name softly as I close my eyes and slowly slip one hand downwards to rub my fingers against my pouting cunney lips. With the other I am fondling my breasts and, aaah, my fingertip has just entered my love channel but how much nicer it would be if it were you who was parting the soft folds of skin.

My hands are now busy, forming circles over my aroused clitty, pressing my blonde bush until I can feel the thrilling flow of an approaching spend. Now my left thumb is slipping inside my moist slit, though it is a poor substitute for your majestic member, and I am pushing two fingers in my cunney to make it nice and wet. It is time now to grasp hold of your gift of the finely crafted comforter based exactly upon your noble stiffstander. Aaah, I am slowly nudging the helmet between my separated cunney lips and in the mirror I can see to the very depths inside my damp, tight honeypot.

Yet as I push this ivory cock further inside my pussey, I can only think of how you dipped your prick into me gently at first and then moved harder and faster just as I am now moving my comforter, rubbing it across my erect little clitty which now throbs and tingles and my cuntal juices are already dripping out onto the sheet. I'm lifting my titties and pressing my breasts together so I can lick my hard little nips and now I'm fucking myself with the dildo at great speed . . . Oh! Oh! Oh! I am coming! Yes! I'm there! Aaah! Aaah! A-h-r-e! Oooh, that was nice, very nice and I'm licking the creamy cum from the dildo which I am pretending is your live, quivering cock . . .

I won't pretend I didn't enjoy this frigging, but believe me, my dearest, nothing in the world can compare with making love to you, lying back on rumpled sheets with a soft pillow underneath my head and being thrilled to the core by the voluptuous sensations aroused by your gorgeous thick cock reaming out my juicy cunney.

Unless I hear otherwise, I will expect to see you on Thursday. I am feeling so randy that I shall make you forgo your usual lobster salad at lunchtime and feed you half a dozen oysters instead!

All my love,
Jenny

Naturally, reading this racy narrative made my cock rise up again but I resisted the temptation to pull out my prick and administer manual relief to my swollen shaft by a quick five knuckle shuffle because I knew that a great deal of serious fucking awaited us all later this evening and in all probability during the next few days. So I closed my eyes and soon I joined Nancy and Henry in the Land of Nod but we woke up well in time to collect our possessions and alight at Leeds where porters took off our luggage and guided us to the platform where the local Harrogate line train had just arrived. There was only a brief wait of about ten minutes before we were on our way again and in half an hour we had arrived at our destination of Knaresborough.

At the station, Crabtree, our chauffeur, was waiting for us with my father's large Lanchester motor car and old Goldhill was also on hand to meet the party and to supervise the loading of our luggage into one of the estate's carts, with the aid of Frederick, a handsome young footman. I could see that Frederick's powerful physique, shown as he heaved the cases into the cart, had caught Nancy's attention.

On our way to Albion Towers, the seat of the Mountjoys since the sixteenth century, we passed through the high road via Starbeck and, like the American cinematographer Frederick Nolan [see *The Intimate Memoirs of An Edwardian Dandy Volume One: Youthful Scandals* for a graphic description of how Rupert assisted in the production of perhaps the first blue flim made in Britain – Editor], my guests marvelled at the superb view of the luxuriant woods, the venerable cottages, the ruined castle and the old church which make up a superb vista.

'Diana Wigmore is one of many artists who have brought out their easels and painted scenes of Knaresborough from the Castle Hill,' I commented, as we trundled down the hill towards the sleepy village of Wharton. 'If we have time, I'll gladly show you round what's left of the castle which has an interesting history. It was to here that the knights fled after murdering Archbishop Becket, and John of Gaunt is believed to have built the Keep. Incidentally, given half a chance, my father will show you the secret passage he discovered twenty years ago leading from the castle yard to the moat.'

'Such a pity it was demolished,' said Nancy sadly. 'When did that happen?'

'In the seventeenth century, during the Civil War when it was in the hands of the Cavaliers, until Fairfax successfully besieged it after the battle of Marston Moor. Four years later it was reduced to ruins by the Roundheads,' I informed her, and Nancy murmured, 'My, that would be ancient history as far as New Yorkers are concerned.'

'Oh, but part of the Parish Church goes back to the twelfth century, the nave to the fifteenth and the tower was built in 1774, just before your Declaration of Independence,' I added, which impressed Nancy even more. Henry, who had stayed with me several times and knew Knaresborough well, chipped in, 'I'll escort you to the Church one morning if we have time, Nancy. Even an atheist like myself can appreciate the naïve beauty of the two full length paintings on wood of Moses and Aaron in the vestry which date from around the middle of the fifteenth century.'

'I may well take up your offer,' mused Nancy thoughtfully, as Crabtree swung into our drive for the half mile run up to our house. My father, Colonel Harold Elton Fortescue Mountjoy, late of the Sixth Bengal Lancers, was standing by the front steps waiting to greet us.

'Hello everyone, welcome to Albion Towers.

Ah, it's Bascombe-Thomas, good to see you again, young man,' he boomed, shaking hands with Henry as we climbed out of the car. 'Now Rupert, you must introduce me to this charming girl who hails from America, does she not?'

'Yes, Father, this is Miss Nancy Carrington of Fifth Avenue, New York City, Nancy, this is Colonel Mountjoy, my father.'

'A pleasure to meet you, my dear young lady. Ah, here comes my wife who has been busying herself all morning with some dashed political meeting about votes for women. Well, being an American, at least you can't be a blooming suffragette, Miss Carrington,' sighed my father, who, though a decent old stick, was still in many ways a crusty old buffer and was genuinely astonished by the 'wild women' who had the temerity to demand equal rights and even more puzzled when two years ago my mother announced that she had joined Mrs Pankhurst's Women's Social and Political Organisation and would be actively canvassing on its behalf around the county.

'No, I don't need to be; in my country women have already secured the vote,' said Nancy, a smile playing around her lips. 'But I must warn you, Colonel Mountjoy, that the British suffragettes have my total support and I did in fact join their march to Trafalgar Square last September.'

'Oh Lord,' he groaned, though in fact he was not that put out by Nancy's declaration of support for my mother's cause, for despite his innate conservatism, if pressed by my mother, my father was forced to admit that there was no logical reason to bar women from having their say as to how the country should be run.

The stones crunched under my feet as I walked across to meet Mama who embraced me warmly and I introduced Nancy to her. 'How nice to meet you, Miss Carrington. And I'm so pleased that I have a further ally to support me if the subject of female suffrage comes up in conversation. Although my husband would not gainsay me in company, his support is at best lukewarm and I have had to rely solely upon Rupert to back me up when reactionaries like our vicar, Reverend Forsyth and Mr Archer, the squire of Wharton, insist on arguing against me on the grounds that women are inherently inferior to men.'

'How perfectly ridiculous, but then can one really expect more from the stupid sex?' said Nancy, which caused Henry to protest, 'I say, steady on Nancy. There are plenty of men who back the idea of sexual equality. Rupert and I do, for a start and there are many more besides.'

'Yes, I suppose we mustn't tar you all with the same brush, though it would be hard indeed to find more silly fools than Messrs Archer and Forsyth,' said my mater with a little chuckle. 'But don't let's stand here, come inside the house and have some tea. Don't worry about your luggage. I have left instructions with Polly so that when Goldhill and Frederick arrive they will know into which rooms they should put the various suitcases.'

'Polly, did you say, Mama? But isn't she just a scullery maid? What's happened to Sally?' I asked anxiously, for though I had fucked both girls, I was especially fond of Sally Tomlinson whose ripe, generous curves were admired by a great many male visitors to Albion Towers from our local medical practitioner Doctor Attenborough to my Uncle Algy (Lord Trippett) who always gave the girl a five pound note for services rendered during his frequent stays with us.

'Sally Tomlinson left us after announcing her engagement to Farmer Harrington's youngest son, Edmund, whom she met whilst he was on leave from his ship,' explained my mother patiently. 'Do you remember Edmund, dear? He joined the merchant navy after deciding that the agricultural life was too staid for his taste,' explained my mother. 'So Sally is staying with her parents in Ripley until his next leave early next month when the marriage ceremony will take place.'

'Gosh, that's a step up the social scale for her, isn't it?' I remarked mischievously. 'Though I don't suppose the Harringtons were exactly overjoyed at the match. Good luck to her, she's a sprightly girl and I'm sure she'll be able to cope with her new position as a naval officer's wife. So meanwhile, I presume that Polly has been promoted to the exalted rank of parlour maid.'

As we walked through into the hall my father looked at me through narrowed eyes and muttered, 'I didn't realise how interested you were in the running of the household, my lad. Mmph, I think it's just as well Sally's left Albion Towers or both you and she might have found yourselves in a spot of bother.'

'I'm sure I don't know what you mean, father,' I

said innocently, but the pater waved away my protestations. 'Don't give me any of that nonsense,' he growled angrily as we followed the others into the drawing room. 'I'm damned sure your Uncle Algy was poking her and I wouldn't put it past you ignoring my advice to keep your hands off the servants.'

Wisely, I did not attempt a denial and was careful not to appear to be over familiar with Polly, the pert girl who now proudly wore a smart housemaid's uniform instead of the drab clothes of a scullery maid. I answered Polly politely when she said, 'Good-afternoon, Mister Rupert, I hope you are keeping well.' However, despite my vow to heed my father's warning about the perils of being too intimate with the servants, I simply could not resist pinching her luscious bottom as she brushed past me carrying a tray of sandwiches. She gave a tiny squeal but thankfully held on to her tray which she offered to Nancy Carrington. When she came to me, she leaned forward and though her loose black uniform prevented a look at her firm breasts, she winked at me and whispered, 'Wait till after dinner, you naughty boy, I'll come up to your room at eleven o'clock.'

There was no opportunity to speak further with Polly so I nodded briefly although I was now in the happy position of having, if anything, an over-abundance of girls laying claim to my cock during these few days at home. Even as I mulled over the situation, my father informed me that Diana Wigmore and her parents would be dining with us tonight. There was also Nancy Carrington to consider, of course, who during the train journey had already extended an invitation to share her bed later in the day and now Polly Aysgarth had as good as demanded to be fucked after dinner!

Then, would you believe it, Goldhill entered the room, and, after announcing that our luggage was all safely in our bedrooms and was being unpacked by Polly and Alison, another new addition to our household who I had not yet seen, our faithful old retainer turned to me and said, 'There is a telephone call for you, sir. Miss Cecily Cardew is on the line.'

'Thank you, Goldhill, I'll take the call straightaway. Please excuse me, everybody,' I said as I hurried into the hall. Cecily, as readers of my first book of uncensored memoirs [*Youthful Scandals* – Editor] will recall, was Diana Wigmore's closest friend, who joyfully helped my best friend Frank Folkestone through his first ever rite-of-passage on a wonderfully sensual afternoon in the old barn near our freshly laid lawn tennis court.

I picked up the telephone and said, 'Hello, Cecily, are you there? Rupert Mountjoy here. How are you keeping?'

'Rupert, hello, how nice to hear your voice. We haven't seen each other since Christmas, have we?'

'No, not since Diana's Old Year's Night party,' I said, and then I almost bit my tongue, for I remembered that to be absolutely exact, the last time I saw Cecily, she was kneeling on the floor of the Wigmore's dining-room (fortunately Diana's parents had decided to stay out until midnight with my folks at Albion Towers), and she was lustily sucking the veiny shaft of Reverend Campbell Armstrong, the curate of Farnham whilst being fucked doggie-style by young Brindleigh Pearce, the seventeen-year-old son of a nearby landowner, whose shining eyes and speed of spending suggested that Cecily had just taken another young man's unwanted virginity.

However, my recollection did not trouble Cecily who carried on, 'Diana has told me all about what you're doing to sell her paintings. You are a good chap, Rupert, let's hope something comes out of all your efforts. And the reason I'm calling is I understand that Henry Bascombe-Thomas is staying with you at Albion Towers. Just before he went to America, Henry and I met at Maureen Waller's coming-out ball and we struck up an immediate friendship although we did not manage to seal our relationship with more than a quick good-night kiss. My parents are away until tomorrow afternoon and I wondered if there was any chance of meeting him tonight?'

'Of course you can, Cecily. Why don't you dine with us? No, really, my parents are always pleased to see you. Anyhow, Diana and her parents are coming over this evening so you could come with them. Will you fix the arrangements with Diana? Good, I look forward to seeing you tonight and I'll tell Henry that he has a pleasant surprise in store. Au revoir till tonight.'

So now there would be a fourth girl who would probably be calling for my cock as Cecily was renowned for enjoying a threesome with her close friends. However, even though I was renowned as a lusty, libidinous fellow who could wield a pulsing prick from dusk to dawn, I was very glad that I would be able to call upon Henry's sturdy stiffstander to help ensure that none of the four girls concerned would have cause to complain of a shortage of stiff cockshaft!

I went back into the drawing-room, but before I could sit down Nancy said to my mother, 'Mrs Mountjoy, would you mind if I went upstairs? I'd like to take a short rest before getting ready for dinner.'

'Of course not, my dear,' replied my mother. 'Please feel quite free to do so. Rupert, perhaps you would kindly escort Miss Carrington to her room.'

'With pleasure, Mama,' I said, little thinking that Nancy had any ulterior motive for wishing to leave the company. After all, I could hardly stay very long with her considering that my parents and Henry were downstairs and it would be very bad form for Nancy and I to be away more than a few minutes together, especially when the others knew that we were in her bedroom.

Therefore I took Nancy upstairs without any trepidation that my prick might be called upon to perform. Now I have no wish to appear blasé, as I've always been game for a good fuck at any time of the day or night, but I honestly wanted to conserve my strength for what I knew would be a strenuous evening ahead. On the other hand, what was I to do when as I stood at the entrance of her bedroom, Nancy bundled me inside and swiftly locked the door? It would have been most impolite to my guest to refuse her the use of my stiffening shaft which she was squeezing deliciously as our lips met in a warm, passionate embrace, especially as I could hardly tell her that she was going to be one of four girls whose cunnies would be competing for my cock in a very short space of time.

In the circumstances, I felt it best to let Nature take its course and made no effort to move away as, quick as a flash, Nancy pulled off her blouse and chemise and knelt bare breasted before me as she hungrily unbuttoned my trousers. The sight of her two snow white spheres tipped with their delicious engorged nipples sent my shaft rising high and my rod was rigid when she opened her mouth and began sucking and licking my uncapped knob.

Nevertheless, I felt it incumbent upon me to warn the dear girl that I could only stay with her a short while. For answer, she held my throbbing tool in both hands and washed my bell-end with her tongue. Then, filling her mouth with saliva, she plunged my prick inside her, withdrew her head back and then bobbed her head forward and backwards, forwards and backwards in a wonderfully sensual manner. Within a minute, the pressure built up in the base of my cock and with a cry I held her head as I heaved my hips forwards, filling her mouth with a fierce fountain of sticky spunk as my shaft shuddered out a copious emission of jism.

Nancy sighed and pouted, 'A short but sweet sucking off like that should be the hors d'oeuvres to an entrée of a jolly good stint of fucking. So I hope you won't let me down, Rupert, and you'll give me your word that after dinner my cunney will be the first to be filled by your lovely thick penis.'

I looked blankly at her and she wagged her finger at me, saying, 'Oh come on, Rupert, I wasn't born yesterday, as we say in New York. I could see you had an eye for Polly, the maid who served us tea, and I'm sure your best chum Diana Wigmore will also be after her share of stiff cockshaft, won't she?'

Well, what could I say to this perpicacious girl? My old headmaster, Dr Keeleigh always advised us in awkward situations 'to tell the truth and shame the devil'. So I decided. 'That is very possible as I haven't seen Diana for some months,' I admitted with a grin as I pushed my still wet semi-stiff prick back into my trousers. 'But on the other hand, I am a firm believer in the maxim of first come, first served so I promise upon my honour as an English gentleman that I will fuck you before anyone else tonight.'

'Anyone else?' she echoed, clapping a hand to her mouth. 'Oh, I suppose you are thinking that Polly will expect to be brought off too.'

In for a penny, in for a pound, I thought, and I said, 'Yes, and in all probability, so will another young lady who you have not yet met who is also dining with us this evening.' And I then told Nancy about the telephone call from Cecily Cardew, hoping that she would not take umbrage at the situation which had now developed.

'Cecily also enjoys a gambol with other girls and I don't think Polly would object to taking part in such encounters either,' I concluded, which made Nancy smile and say, 'In that case, you had better go back downstairs, Rupert, and I'll take a rest so as to be fit for the fray.

'Just do me one small favour, Rupert, don't indulge yourself too much at dinner tonight, especially as far as alcohol is concerned, and please ask Henry to be similarly abstemious when it comes to passing the port after the ladies have left the table. Remember what the Bard of Avon had to say about drinking – it makes and mars, sets you on and takes you off, persuades and disheartens, and provokes the desire but takes away the performance!'

'Don't worry yourself on that score,' I assured the lovely Yankee miss. 'Henry and I would far rather get laid than get drunk,' I assured her. 'We usually dine at eight so why don't we meet in the lounge at seven o'clock for a pre-dinner drink?

'I'll have fresh apple juice which Mrs Randall our cook always has on hand,' I added hastily, as I kissed her proferred cheek and went out onto the landing where Polly passed by me carrying a pile of clean towels.

'Hello, Rupert,' she said softly, as she brushed her hip against my groin. 'Don't forget now that I'll be in your room at eleven o'clock and I might have a nice little surprise for you. But don't worry, I've already taken off my knickers and I'm looking forward to milking your thick prick all night. Just as well it's my day off tomorrow so I don't have to get up too early.'

I gave the frisky girl a glassy smile before running downstairs and just as I was about to open the door of the drawing-room, old Goldhill called out to me from across the hall. 'Just one minute, sir, if you please, I must speak to you.'

His tone sounded urgent so I said with slight irritation, 'What is it, Goldhill? Can't it possibly wait till later? I'm in a bit of a hurry just now.'

'Sorry, Mister Rupert, I won't keep you long but it is a rather important matter,' said the butler, as he hurried across to me and lowered his voice. 'Look, sir, I think you should know that Alison, our new housemaid, celebrates her eighteenth birthday tomorrow. She has taken a great shine to you and she has told me that the nicest present of all would be being fucked by Mister Rupert whenever he has a spare hour or two.'

Another honeypot to be sampled! Now whilst I was flattered to be fancied by a girl who I had not yet even clapped eyes upon, the forthcoming evening was threatening to get out of control! I steeled myself to tell Goldhill that Alison would have to wait her turn when a mop of bright blonde hair appeared around the corner of the door leading to the kitchen and scullery. The owner of this tousled mass then showed her face for a couple of moments and Goldhill called out, 'Very well, Alison, I'll be with you very shortly.'

All thoughts of postponing my prick's appointment with the new maid fled rapidly from my brain for Alison was quite stunningly pretty with cornflower blue eyes, a tiny nose but with generously wide red lips and I caught a glimpse of her smile which showed off two pearly white rows of teeth. So I said to Goldhill, 'I'll try to fit Alison in after dinner tonight. Please tell her to come to my room just before midnight. But I've never even met the girl and she can only have seen me for a few moments this afternoon, so I'm rather puzzled as to why she has been so attracted to me.'

The silver-haired servant scratched his head and said, 'To be truthful, sir, I didn't ask, but my guess is that her appetite has been whetted by Polly who never tires of talking in some detail about the uproarious night with you and Master Frank Folkestone some years ago when she was a mere slip of a girl.'

A slow smile crept over his face and I also chuckled as I said, 'Well, she may have only been sweet sixteen but by Jove, she was far more experienced than either of us. In fact, if my memory serves me right, we first encountered Polly Aysgarth when she was bending over the scullery table with your John Thomas pressed between her luscious bum cheeks.'

'Very true, sir, Polly adores fucking although I have never had the pleasure of conjoining with her again as she is well-served by some lusty young bucks in the village. Actually, soon after the event you have just mentioned, she went down to London to serve in Lord Borehamwood's town house in Belgravia. But she did not enjoy the experience and your mother was kind enough to take her back about six months later.'

'Oh yes, of course, Mama did mention it in a letter whilst I was up in Oxford. I was surprised when I heard the news because Polly always wanted to go to London. Do you know why she came back here?'

Goldhill cleared his throat and murmured, 'I understand that his lordship has somewhat strange tastes when it comes to intimate affairs. Apparently most of his loves are of the homosexualist variety, although he did occasionally take a girl to bed. But his demands were very odd – the only way he could achieve an erection was if Polly dressed up like a schoolboy and caned his bare behind. Even then, all he wanted was for her to suck him. He never fucked her all the time she was in his service.'

'What very odd behaviour,' I agreed as I pushed open the drawing-room door, 'especially when there's an eager, willing wench like Polly on hand. Anyhow, Goldhill, don't forget to tell Alison to come for her birthday present just before midnight and she'll see that at Albion Towers we don't have such nonsense as poor Polly had to put up with in London.'

'Ah, there you are, Rupert,' said my father crossly as I entered the drawing-room. 'Your mother was about to send out a search party.'

'Sorry to have been so long but I was just giving Nancy the usual lecture on the more interesting aspects of local history,' I said, making for the whisky which stood on a silver salver on the sideboard.

'An oral lesson, eh? I wonder who was the teacher and who was the pupil,' muttered Henry, who was standing by me.

'Don't fret, Henry, you'll find out for yourself later on,' I advised him cheerfully. 'Can I offer anyone a drink?'

'No, thank you dear,' said my mother, rising to

her feet. 'I suggest you drink only soda or you can ask Polly to bring you some more tea. We'll dine at the usual time and your father has favoured us with the best bottles in the cellar to complement Mrs Randall's excellent cooking, haven't you, dear?'

My father grunted, 'Well, I've done my best to provide something worth drinking. We'll start with champagne, and, for those who prefer to change to a non-sparkling wine for the fish course, there'll be a 1902 Pinot Blanc – I've already told Goldhill to chill half a dozen bottles in the ice-box. I'm putting out the last of the chateau bottled Beaune from Count Gewirtz's vineyards which will go splendidly with the beef and there'll be a sweet wine, of course, afterwards for the desserts. We'll serve that 1903 Chateau d'Yquem I bought last time we were in Bordeaux.

'So it would be foolish to begin imbibing heavily before dinner,' he said meaningfully with a disapproving look in my direction.

I accepted the implied rebuke and splashed some plain soda into a glass as my mother said to me, 'By the way, dear, I forgot to mention that your Aunt Penelope will also be joining us for dinner. Unfortunately, as Uncle Stephen has been called to London on business, she will come alone and stay the night here. And that reminds me, I'd better make sure her bedroom is ready.'

My father looked less than ecstatic at the news and after my parents left the room, Henry said, 'Your father gave the impression that he was hardly overjoyed at the news of an extra guest, although you looked far more pleased to hear than an old aunt was dining with you.'

'Ah well, for a start, Aunt Penelope isn't old. She's a very attractive woman in her mid-forties and about ten years younger than her husband, Uncle Stephen. And she's not an aunt in the strict sense of the word. Penelope and Stephen Trelford-Neil are perhaps my parents' closest friends and I grew up with Alicia and Georgina, their twin daughters, although I haven't seen the girls since they went to Italy last year for an extended stay with Uncle Stephen's brother who is the commercial attaché at our embassy in Rome.

'Aunt Penelope is a keen amateur artist and I suppose my mother thought that she would be interested to meet you and Nancy. I like her very much and I'm sure you'll also enjoy her company. My father has always admired Aunt Penelope (in fact I think he harbours naughty ideas about her) but since she has also become a keen member of the women's suffrage movement, he and Uncle Stephen tend to drown their sorrows together whilst my mother and Aunt Penelope go round the county drumming up support for votes for women.'

'She sounds a feisty lady and I look forward to meeting her,' said Henry and, after I had swallowed down my soda, we went upstairs to prepare for dinner.

'You've never mentioned your Aunt's twin daughters,' said Henry suddenly, pausing at the entrance of his bedroom. 'Have you been keeping some wicked secrets from me as far as they are concerned? Having a pretty set of twins together is one of my unfulfilled fantasies.'

I laughed and said, 'In that case you would be even more frustrated if you ever met Alicia and Georgina. They are only nineteen years old and although not identical twins, they do look very much alike.'

'And are the two girls both attractive?' he asked.

'Absolutely ravishing, old boy, but I've never had the opportunity to progress further than a kiss under the mistletoe at Christmas parties,' I said regretfully, as it had been my ambition to bed the heavenly twins.

On this wistful note I left Henry and went to my own bedroom where the young footman, Frederick, whose duties also included basic valeting for my father and any male guests, had unpacked my cases, hung up some clothes in the wardrobe and had laid out my best evening suit which Mr Rabinowitz made for me when I came down from Oxford. The black barathea cloth was almost as smooth as the silk collar and lapels. It would set off the sparkling new stiff shirt and cuff links I had been given by Mama for my birthday which I would wear for the first time tonight.

I ran a bath and enjoyed a luxurious soak before drying myself off in front of the mirror, feeling refreshed and pleased with life. As I passed the towel between my legs I thought of the grand festival of fucking that awaited my pleasure after dinner and I idly imagined how nice it would have been to have started the affair by being sucked off by Alicia and Georgina Trelford-Neil.

These lewd thoughts combined with the pressure of the towel on my cock caused my shaft to spring to life and in a trice it was standing rigidly to attention up against my belly. Now, perhaps I had not heard a knock on the bedroom door because of the swirling gurgle of the bath-water disappearing down the plug hole, but as I was lightly stroking my proud prick, I was startled to hear a discreet little cough from the bathroom doorway – and when I looked up to see who was there, I was only partially relieved to see that it was only Polly standing there, for whilst she would be pleased rather than scandalised to see my erect naked prick, on the other hand, I honestly wanted to conserve my strength for later. Though from the gleam in Polly's eyes, I could tell that her blood was up and it would be difficult to deny her a taste of her favourite lollipop!

It was then with a resigned pleasure that I dropped the towel and stood with my legs slightly apart as Polly dropped to her knees and clasped her warm, soft fingers around my prick. She cupped my ballsack with her other hand as if weighing the contents in her palm whilst she frigged my swollen shaft.

'Do you like having me play with your cock and balls, Mister Rupert?' she whispered and all I could do was to nod my head as by now my heart was pounding and my whole body was thrilling to the sensations afforded by Polly's skilful fingers.

'Well, if that's the case, let's see what you think of this,' she said decisively and leaned right forward to take my throbbing cock and encase my knob inside her hot, wet mouth. Her darting tongue moved to and fro along my shaft and, as she sucked on her cocksweet, I felt my balls begin to swell and fill with sperm. Frenziedly, I thrust forwards and backwards between her lips and I must have transmitted my urgency to Polly because she began to suck harder and harder, letting my prick slide thickly against her tongue whilst she squeezed my balls.

I groaned as a rush of creamy spunk sped along my stem and jetted out into her mouth. She gulped down as much of my jism as she could but Polly simply could not contend with the tremendous gush I produced. My copious emission dripped down her chin and onto her blouse and after finally milking my cock of the final drains of sticky sperm, she kissed my now flaccid staff, wiped the jism off her blouse and sucked her fingers clean.

'Goodness, my blouse is damp and I'm soaking wet between my legs,' she said. 'Look for yourself, I told you as you were leaving Miss Carrington's room that I've already taken off my knickers.' And she immediately proved the truth of this remark by pulling down her skirt and lifting her blouse and chemise to reveal the dark patch of pubic hair adorning her sweet little cunt.

The sight of Polly's pussey coupled with thoughts of anticipation of what was scheduled to occur after dinner made my tadger tingle and it began to swell up again. Heroically, I passed up the opportunity for a quick knee-trembler, and I picked up the towel and wrapped it around my waist.

'Polly, there just isn't time to fuck you right now,' I said firmly. 'Please be a good girl and come back here around eleven o'clock. Then, as I've told you, I will have more time to pay your lovely cunney the close attention it richly deserves.'

This little speech seemed to mollify Polly and she put her skirt back on, saying, 'Yes, we certainly don't want to rush things. After all, as Goldhill's already told you, you also have to keep Alison satisfied all night and she's a very passionate girl.'

I hurried her to the door and when she closed it behind her I sank down upon the bed for a brief snooze. But I found it hard to sleep because I was very worried as to how I would be able to do my duty by Nancy, Polly, and Alison – as well as by Diana and Cecily who would soon be arriving downstairs! Henry would put his trusty tool at my disposal but I reckoned that I still needed one more cock to ensure that none of the girls was disappointed by the arrangements for their entertainment.

In the end, I did manage forty winks before it was time to change for dinner. I walked downstairs at about half past seven to find Nancy and my parents already engaged in conversation with Diana's parents, Charles and Helene Wigmore.

'Good-evening, Rupert,' said Mrs Wigmore, as I entered the drawing-room. 'How nice to see you again. Are you enjoying your sabbatical year in London?'

'I'll say he is, Helene,' interrupted Dr Wigmore

with a short laugh. 'After all, he has nothing else to do with himself, has he?'

'You're just jealous, sir,' I smiled, accepting a cup of punch from Frederick who was serving my Mama's excellent recipe from a large silver bowl.

'You're quite right, Rupert, I admit it,' cried our neighbour and family medical practitioner, pointing towards Nancy. 'Especially when I'm told you have this charming young lady as your neighbour.'

'Well, Rupert and I are almost neighbours, I suppose, as we both live in Bedford Square,' said Nancy, coming over to us. 'But I'm also fortunate in having such a friendly gentleman living nearby.'

'Ah, my daughter has just come in,' said Dr Wigmore, as Diana and Cecily Cardew made their entrance. As always, the girls looked simply stunning together: the blonde Diana's cool, lissome beauty was exquisitely complemented by the equally pretty Cecily's wavy brown hair, rosy cheeks, large dark eyes and rich red lips.

Dr Wigmore was about to introduce the girls to Nancy when Henry suddenly appeared, so I took on the job for him. Just as I had finished, Goldhill sonorously announced the arrival of Mrs Trelford-Neil and this time my mother came across to perform a similar function for Aunt Penelope although, as my mother remarked, only Henry and Nancy were strangers to her.

'I dislike that word, Veronica,' said Aunt Penelope. 'As the Irish poet says, there are no strangers in the world, there are only new friends I have yet to meet.'

Aunt Penelope was one of those people whom hostesses loved, for without hogging the limelight herself, she was often the life and soul of a party. She was adept at finding subjects of interest for lively conversation as well as for drawing out shy guests and ensuring that they were not left out in the cold.

So, very soon, she had elicited the fact that both Henry and Nancy were in the market for paintings and she said to them, 'I suppose I should offer you a selection of my water-colours. My husband would probably faint clean away if I informed him that I'd actually sold one of my studies of Knaresborough Castle! But seriously, I paint solely for my own pleasure, whilst Diana here is a talented young professional artist who has a great future in front of her.'

'Mrs Trelford-Neil is one of my staunchest fans,' explained Diana, who had glided gracefully towards us. 'In all fairness, I must tell you that her opinion of my work is hopelessly biased.'

'Nonsense,' Aunt Penelope declared. 'I confidently predict that your portrait of my husband will one day be hung in the Royal Academy.' [This prophecy was fulfilled in 1912 when Diana Wigmore's portrait of Sir Stephen Trelford-Neil (he was ennobled in 1913) was shown at the Academy's Summer Exhibition. Alas, many of Diana Wigmore's works were lost when enemy action destroyed the Allendale Gallery during the London Blitz of 1940 – Editor]

Goldhill called us in to the dining-room and during the meal much of the conversation around my corner of the room revolved around twentieth-century art. I was glad to see that Nancy and Henry were obviously impressed by Diana's knowledge and enthusiasm which boded well for the time when they would cast critical eyes on her own canvases.

'I have just had a splendid idea,' Henry announced excitedly. 'Rupert, why don't you help Diana and myself organise an exhibition in London of the French impressionists – a mix, let us say, of famous fellows like Matisse, Van Gogh and Gaugin with equally talented artists who are not as well-known over in England. As Diana is based in Paris, we would have someone on the spot to choose paintings for us from the new avant-garde.'

'That's quite an undertaking,' I said doubtfully. 'The cost would be considerable and it would take a great deal of time to organise.'

'Well, you're not doing very much these days,' called out my father, who had caught the drift of this conversation, 'so you've enough time to lend a hand.'

'Finance wouldn't necessarily present a problem,' said Henry. 'I don't believe it would cost a fortune to hire a gallery early next Spring and we would pay Rupert his travelling expenses as a nominal honorarium.'

Now whilst I would stoutly defend myself against any accusation of being a Philistine regarding artistic affairs, initially the idea of spending my precious free months working on setting up an exhibition of modern paintings was hardly of great appeal. But then I realised that such a position would give me ample opportunity to visit Diana in Paris – and my trip would be paid for, in the bargain!

My eyes brightened even further when Diana said, 'What a wonderful idea, Henry. I know that you and Rupert would judge potential exhibitors solely upon the quality of their work for there are several girls I know who are held back simply because their sex precludes them from being shown at the best commercial galleries.'

'Don't begin talking about downtrodden women again, Diana,' said Dr Wigmore teasingly. 'I am sure that Colonel Mountjoy agrees with me that this subject is becoming tiresome through constant repetition.'

Diana smiled but my mother took the bait and bristled, 'Charles, the subject will need constant repetition. Only last week I came across a small but pertinent example of blatent sexual discrimination. You may know that Mrs Anna Kempster, who has supervised the Yorkshire School Boards for many years, retired this year. Her co-chairman, Mr Spencer Arbuthnot, has received an OBE in the King's Birthday Honours list, whilst Anna's name was conspicuous by its absence.'

'Actually, that's not a good example, Veronica,' said my father. 'Arbuthnot didn't get his gong for his work on the School Boards. His gift of five thousand pounds to Conservative Party funds earned him his medal.'

'How disgraceful,' remarked Cecily Cardew, who was sitting next to me but had said little during the meal. 'Such sordid horse-trading makes the list a parody of honour and an insult to those members of the community who truly merit recognition.'

'Well, whilst I can't reasonably defend the system, my dear,' my father said, 'you must admit it keeps Civil Servants happy and loyal to the government of the day and hopefully some decent chaps do get their just rewards for selfless service. As for politics, it's a dirty business but party funds need replenishing and I suppose selling baubles is as good a way as any to top up the accounts.'

'Maybe so, but it is indefensible that membership of the House of Lords should be decided by accident of birth,' said Cecily, a sentiment which earned a murmur of approval from all but my father and Dr Wigmore who shrugged their shoulders and muttered something about the need for an officer class in society.

When the ladies left the table and Frederick came in with the port and cognac, the two old codgers continued their objections to twentieth-century standards and the passing of the old ways. Henry and I listened in silence, giving each other an occasional conspiratorial wink. After all, there was little point trying to change their views, although when Dr Wigmore opined that what this country needed was 'a few people to give the orders and the rest to obey them pretty smartish!' Henry mouthed a muttered suggestion as to where Dr Wigmore should next stick his stethescope!

Anyhow, our minds were concentrated upon more immediate matters to hand and when my father suggested that we rose and joined the ladies, we took up his remark with alacrity. When we rejoined the girls, Diana said to me, 'Rupert, would you and Cecily like to accompany Henry, Nancy and myself to the library? Your mother has my portrait of her hanging there and has kindly agreed that I should show it to our guests.'

I looked enquiringly at my mother who said, 'By all means, Rupert, and then do feel free to adjourn to the games room. Perhaps you young people might enjoy a game of billiards or table tennis whilst we old fogies sit down to a game of bridge.'

We thanked Mama for her considerate thought and trouped out towards the library. But in the hallway, Cecily laid her hand on my arm and said, 'Rupert, why don't we leave Diana to show Nancy and Henry the painting by herself? They can talk amongst themselves about the pre-Raphaelites, the post-impressionists and whatever artistic gossip they choose without worrying about us.'

'What a good idea,' said Henry approvingly. 'We'll meet you later in the games-room.'

'Or if we don't find you there, Diana, Henry and I will make tracks for your bedroom and come straight in without knocking on the door,' warned Nancy jokingly, although I knew that she was totally serious about taking such a drastic course of action!

Anyhow, we agreed to split up and when the library doors closed upon the three artistic aficionados, Cecily rubbed the palm of her hand suggestively against my prick and said, 'You know, Rupert, I do believe that Nancy meant what she said about flinging open your bedroom door, so why don't we adjourn there now. That way we might actually be able to meet them in the games-room later!'

I looked at my watch and saw it was almost twenty minutes to eleven and it occurred to me that not only would it be delicious to make love to this gorgeous girl but if Cecily Cardew's love channel was the first to be crammed full of my cock, this would solve a tricky problem which had been bothering me. For even though fucking Cecily first meant I would be breaking my promise to Nancy and Diana, both of them knew of each other's desire to have me fuck them, but this way, by first favouring Cecily's neutral pussey, so to speak, neither Polly nor Diana would have cause to feel any jealousy towards one another.

Perhaps I might abandon law and try my hand at diplomacy, I thought to myself as I opened the door to my bedroom for Cecily. I was swiftly shaken out of any smugness, however, because as I closed and was about to lock the door, it became apparent that someone had filched the key!

Which girl had taken it? Probably Nancy, I reasoned, as I responded to Cecily's advances and kissed her on the lips, although I would not have put it past Polly to have slipped the key into her pocket when she left me just before dinner.

Unfortunately, it became obvious to Cecily that something was on my mind for she said reproachfully, 'Rupert, what's the matter with you?'

'Nothing, nothing at all,' I reassured her and swept her into my arms. But the nagging question still ran through my mind and Cecily broke away from me and began to undress until she stood naked in front of me. 'Now then, Rupert Mountjoy,' she said crossly, as she pirouetted round in a circle, 'do you like the merchandise or would you prefer to have it wrapped up and sent back to the shop?'

I gazed upon her soft, white body, now totally nude and of such ravishing beauty that almost unconsciously I licked my lips in anticipation. Cecily was a real corker and when she unpinned her hair and let the silky strands fall over her shoulders onto her large breasts, I would have challenged any red-blooded man in the world not to have had his cock standing stiffly in salute. I looked down and smiled as she ran her fingers across the curly brown bush between her legs and pulled open the pouting love lips to reveal the pink chink of her cunney.

'Certainly not, I wish to make a purchase,' I croaked as she took three paces forward and helped me off with my jacket.

'You will?' she cooed happily, transferring her attentions to my fly buttons. 'I hope you won't change your mind and look elsewhere half-way through the transaction.'

'No I won't,' I panted heavily as I sat down on the bed and Cecily assisted me to remove my shoes. 'Though if necessary I promise that I'll leave a deposit and come back later to complete the sale.'

Within a very short space of time I was also naked and all extraneous matters like the missing key and who might come in whilst Cecily and I were enjoying our naked romp fled from my mind. Cecily opened her legs and I buried my face in the damp patch of curly cunney moss. 'Make love to my cunt, Rupert,' she whispered, and, nothing loath, I began to kiss her salivating pussey lips and started to lick her hairy crack in long lascivious swipes of my tongue. The vermilion lips parted and between them I felt her stiffened clitty which I rolled around in my mouth.

'Oooh! Oooh! A-h-r-e!' she cried out, her body threshing from side to side as she rolled her thighs around my neck. 'Suck me off, darling, make me come with your wicked little tongue!'

I sucked away at an ever-increasing speed, rolling my tongue round and round her clitty, nipping it occasionally with my teeth which made her squeal with ecstasy and I licked up Cecily's tangy love juices in great gulps as she began to spend. Her entire frame was caught up into a giant shudder and then a fine creamy emission spurted from her cunney, flooding my mouth with a salty essence, which I lapped up until she shivered into limpness as the delicious crisis melted away.

'Please fuck me now,' she breathed and naturally I was happy to fulfil her demand, moving my body upwards so our lips met as my swollen knob slipped in between the portals of her rubbery pussey lips, straight into her sopping cunt. I moved my head downwards to suck on her firm, tawny nipples which made her gasp with delight and I fucked Cecily with great ardour, plunging my prick in and out of her sopping pussey, my balls banging against her backside as my shaft slid all the way inside her and our pubic hairs mingled damply together.

By Jove, Cecily was a grand fuck! How tightly her pussey clasped my rampant cock and how luscious was the suction created by the folds of her juicy cunt as my trusty tool embedded itself inside her slippery sheath. How voluptuously she met my thrusts with the most energetic heaves as we gave ourselves up to an all-enveloping feast of lascivious delights.

Then it struck me that I must ration my fucking if I were ever to get through the night, so I made no attempt to hold back the ultimate pleasure when I felt the spunk boiling up in my balls. With a groan I exploded into a huge climactic release as I shot my load of hot, sticky spunk deep into the lovely girl's cunney which I could feel throb as my cock spurted jet after jet of jism inside her, lubricating her love channel as we went off together. For some moments neither of us moved. We lay there huffing and panting in each other's arms, luxuriating in the utter bliss of it all.

About five minutes later, Cecily turned to me and said, 'Now I know you must want to fuck Diana and she had already told me how much she wants your big boner between her legs. Now I would be the first to admit that as Diana is your closest girl friend, she is entitled to first claim on your darling cock – but she's not here yet, although she did take the precaution of coming upstairs and popping your bedroom key in her handbag when we left you men to pass the port.

So it was Diana who had taken my key! I made a mental apology to Nancy and Polly as I heard

Cecily continue, 'On the other hand, speaking as one of her oldest friends, I can also say that she would have no objection whatsoever to you fucking me again in her absence.'

Without waiting for my reply, the insatiable girl took hold of my limp shaft and in seconds had frigged it up to another bursting erection. Then she rolled over on her elbows and knees with her head on the pillow and her white, rounded bum cheeks stuck high in the air. I climbed up and parted the soft globes with my hands though I hesitated a moment before plunging my prick in the crevice between the fleshy spheres. Cecily guessed what was in my mind and turned her head round and panted, 'Yes, yes, Rupert, do go on. I have a great fancy for a bottom fuck but please go carefully.'

As she wriggled her bum to an even higher angle and opened her legs still wider, I placed my knob, which was still wet from our previous encounter, at the rim of the puckered little rosette. I angled her legs to afford a better view and then gently eased my knob forward and mounted her, sliding my shaft in and out of her rear dimple whilst I squeezed her tits in my hands. I didn't manage to reach another climax myself (which in the circumstances didn't bother me too much) but thankfully Cecily began gasping and moaning as I finished her off by tickling her pussey with my fingers.

I withdrew my cock carefully from her puckered bum-hole and we lay together on the bed and I cuddled Cecily tightly in my arms. Frankly, we were now both ready for a short rest

– remember, we'd consumed a delicious dinner not all that long before – but just as we were sliding into the arms of Morpheus, who should sidle quietly into the room but Polly and Alison, who both wore dressing gowns with, as I correctly guessed, nothing on underneath.

'Hello Mister Rupert, who's that with you? Oh, it's Miss Cecily, isn't it? Goodness me, young sir,' she said saucily, in the kind of stately deferential tone beloved of butlers like old Goldhill. 'Do Miss Diana and that nice American lady, Miss Carrington, know you've already started shafting? I last saw them half an hour ago when they were being fucked by Mr Henry in the library but I'm sure I heard one of them say that she wanted to be fucked by you later on. But you did tell me that you would give Alison a special eighteenth birthday present, and come to think of it, I was promised a fuck as well.'

'Is this right, Rupert? Did you promise to fuck these girls?' demanded Cecily, sitting up but making no attempt to hide her luscious naked body.

I nodded miserably, but to my great relief, the sweet girl was not annoyed. 'In that case, you must stick to your word,' she said as an amused smile played around her lips. '*Noblesse oblige*, you know. Whilst you three are occupied, I'll run a bath.'

She swung her legs over the side of the bed and smiling at Polly and Alison, said, 'I hope you're not too disappointed at finding that Rupert has already fucked me.'

'Not at all, Miss Cecily, first come, first served,'

said Polly politely and Cecily added, 'Well, I must admit that I'm glad I was first in the queue but I'm sure Rupert has lots of spunk left in his balls for you and Alison.'

'Thank you, Miss Cecily, you're a real lady to give up a nice thick prick to two servant girls,' said Polly, and she and Alison both curtsied as Cecily heaved herself up and walked across the room into the bathroom, closing the door behind her.

Polly slipped off her robe and as I had guessed, the dressing-gown was her only clothing and the pert parlour maid now stood stark naked in front of me. I feasted my eyes and drank in the sensual beauty of her proud, uptilted breasts, flat white belly and the trimmed tuft of dark pubic hair through which peeped her pink cunney lips.

Yet despite this stirring sight, my prick failed to stand fully to attention, stirring only slightly against my thigh. I leaned forward to take it in my hand and frig my cock up to its full majestic height but Polly removed my fingers which had already closed around my semi-erect shaft.

'Mister Rupert, your cock would prefer to wait a few more minutes before charging back into action,' she said wisely. 'Alison and I are in no rush. Why don't you just move over and we'll amuse ourselves until you're fully ready for us.'

This was sensible advice so I wriggled over and Polly sat down next to me as she motioned Alison to come forward and stand beside her. She then tugged at the sash of Alison's robe, which opened and the gorgeous young girl stepped out of her gown in all her naked glory like a glorious statue come magically to life.

What a truly delectable, enchanting sight! Her creamy white skin showed off her full curvy breasts to their best advantage and her well-rounded shoulders tapered down to a small waist; her dainty feet expanded upwards into fine calves and her marble thighs were beautifully proportioned, whilst hanging between them was a golden veil of curly blonde hairs over a pouting crack which simply begged to be kissed, sucked and fucked.

Not surprisingly, the sight of this cute little cunney made my prick shoot up back to bursting point and I would certainly have replied in the affirmative when Alison spoke for the first time and in a sweet little voice said: 'What a nice, big stiffstander, sir. Did I make your prick swell? I can hardly wait to have you slide it inside my pussey, but would you mind if Polly and I get ourselves warmed-up first?'

'No, not at all, Alison, please carry on,' I croaked and Polly drew the trembling girl down onto the bed between the two of us and parted her thighs. 'You lucky girl, you're going to be fucked very shortly,' she said softly. 'Mister Rupert, look closely at this lovely creature. Just look at her flushed, aroused face, her stiff tawny titties and her luscious cunney. Isn't she simply divine?'

The two girls embraced and slipped their arms around each other's waists in a loose, almost casual hug which quickly tightened and brought their breasts and bellies fiercely into contact. Alison tilted her head and raised her mouth to Polly's lips and closed her eyes expectantly. Her hands quivered as they pressed hotly into the base of Polly's back and the more experienced girl looked down on the lovely, breathless girl, studying the intense desire which was etched upon Alison's face as she yielded to her natural instincts.

At first they kissed like sisters, their red lips meeting in a tentative brushing which gradually deepened into a far more urgent, passionate pressure as their bodies rubbed sensually together. Polly's mouth opened and she probed with the tip of her tongue, sliding it slowly but insistently between Alison's teeth in an inquisitive caress around her gums. This delicious oral stimulation aroused Alison to a sudden, overwhelming passion and her hands slid feverishly up and down Polly's back. This sensuous massage set Polly off and she shuddered violently, thrusting her breasts and pussey forward as she darted her tongue backwards and forwards inside Alison's mouth.

Now Polly cleverly arranged the younger girl's position, making her lie partly on her right side facing me. Her right leg was pushed out almost straight and her left one was drawn up with the heel of her foot being hooked behind Polly's neck as she pressed her face against Alison's wonderful blonde fringed pussey and taking a deep breath, she inhaled the pungent pussey odour. Polly rested her left cheek on Alison's thigh as she slid her left arm under her waist, leaving her right hand to toy with Alison's nut brown pointed nipples. Then when both had settled into the most comfortable position, Polly pressed the gentlest of kisses on Alison's cunney, now and then letting the very tip of her tongue glide between the moistening love lips.

I now scrambled onto my knees and peered down at the thrilling scenario. The serrated lips of Alison's exquisite cunney parted as Polly now thrust her tongue more sharply between them and tongued along the sopping slit whilst now Alison's clitty popped out, as big as a boy's thumb. Polly passed her tongue lasciviously over the rounded ball and nipped at it playfully with her teeth. This made Alison cry out with joy as she tore wildly at the sheets, dragging her body across the bed as Polly stayed with her, her mouth glued tenaciously to Alison's juicy cunt.

This lewd orgiastic display sent me frantic with unslaked desire and I moved quickly behind Polly and slid my shaft in the crevice between her rounded buttocks straight into her own well-oiled honeypot. My hips jerked back and forth whilst I fucked the delicious girl doggie-style, and as my prick slicked in and out of Polly's pussey, I frigged her swollen, erect nipples between my fingers.

But Alison had seen me get behind Polly and she cried out, 'Oh, sir, you did promise that you'd fuck me first!'

Polly lifted her head from Alison's pussey and said thickly, 'Alison's right, Mister Rupert, you had better go on and take my place, but hurry as she's almost ready to spend.'

She rolled off Alison and quick as a flash I took her place, kissing the quivering young girl as I said, 'Happy birthday, Alison, I hope you enjoy your present.' For reply she slipped her hands around my bum cheeks and gripped them as she pushed her glorious breasts up against my chin and manoeuvred one up to my lips. Naturally I bent down and sucked it up inside my mouth as her hands now roamed all over my body, setting my skin on fire. I moved my tongue downwards, drawing circles across her belly even further downwards to her soft blonde nest of cunney hair. Dipping my face close, I licked my fingers and separated the folds, sniffing up the tangy cuntal aroma and lapping up the love juice which Polly's ministrations had already caused to flow. Spreading her cunney lips with my tongue, I explored for a moment, gauging her responses. Then, sliding my arms round her thighs I adjusted my position and tongued her in long flowing licks, flicking her engorged clitty, pushing against the hood.

My tongue moved quickly along her crack as I licked and lapped the tasty juices which now filled my mouth and she let out yelps of delight as she reached the pinnacle of erotic ecstasy.

'Oooh! Oooh! Oooh!' she squealed as I lifted my head and raised myself over her, holding my painfully stiff prick as I guided the knob towards its juicy haven and I delighted in an exquisite pleasure when my helmet parted her cunney lips and I slowly but firmly inserted my throbbing tool inside her slippery sheath. I slid my shaft forward until I was buried up to my balls in Alison's cunt and at first I lay quite still, savouring the feel of the velvety walls of her love channel, as she began to move her hips sinuously, discovering that she could work her cunt up and down my cock with ease as I began to pump up and down and my balls smacked a fine dance against her bottom with every thrust. I pounded to and fro into her squishy cunney, my hands gripping her luscious bum cheeks, as now, at the urging of Polly, I lifted my legs so she could snuggle under my thighs with her head on the sheet and begin sucking my balls whilst she reached down to frig her cunney with her fingers.

Of course, this extra icing on the cake soon sent the surge of spunk shooting up my stem, but by great effort I managed to delay the exquisite moment as the clinging muscles of Alison's cunt continued to sleek back and forth along my sated shaft. However, I would challenge even Sir Clive Bull, perhaps the most noted cocksman south of the Border, to have held back any longer – I certainly could not for more than a few seconds and with a mighty groan I flooded Alison's love hole with a torrent of creamy jism as the sticky essence poured out of my prick, completely filling her cunney and trickling down her inner thighs whilst she screamed out in joy as a huge orgasm shuddered through her delicious body.

'Congratulations, Rupert! Well fucked, sir!' came a familiar female voice from the side of the bed and I looked up to see that the speaker was none other than Diana who had quietly entered the bedroom with Henry and Nancy whilst I had been in the throes of the above described threesome with Alison and Polly.

'Oh Rupert, you did promise me to fuck me first tonight,' said Nancy reproachfully. 'I suppose it's my own fault for getting too carried away with Henry, though I'm sure you will not cavil at my being fucked by your old friend.'

'Not in the slightest, Nancy,' I replied with genuine relief. 'I'm only too pleased that you have been enjoying yourself – but what about you, Diana? I hope that you haven't been left out in the cold.'

'Certainly not,' Henry interrupted indignantly. 'What kind of chap do you take me for? Any man worth his salt would give his right arm for a chance to fuck a beautiful girl like Diana.'

Diana gave a little mock-curtsey and said, 'Thank you, Henry, how sweet of you to say so. You were pretty good in bed yourself and I'm not just saying that because you bought three of my paintings for your proposed New York exhibition of young artists.'

This was good news indeed and there was even better to come. 'Yes, and I purchased Diana's portrait of Sir Louis Segal and also two of her landscapes of Knaresborough Castle,' Nancy chipped in, 'so I think Diana is a very happy young lady.'

'And she certainly deserves to be,' came Cecily's voice from behind the group which slightly startled them. 'Oh, I'm sorry, I didn't mean to make you jump ... There's just one thing wrong here, though,' she added with a twinkle in her eye. 'Why are you three dressed whilst the rest of us are naked?'

'That's good thinking, darling,' said Diana, hastily unbuttoning her dress. 'Move over, Rupert, I think that Cecily would like to congratulate me in her very own special way.'

It took only moments for Diana to undress and everyone in the room thrilled at the sight of her superb lissome nakedness. Diana looked the very acme of feminine perfection, and when she raised her arms to pin up her tresses of light ash blonde hair around her graceful neck, the sight of her proud, firm breasts sent my cock shooting up, and Polly reached over and grabbed my thick stalk, manipulating my foreskin to uncap my swollen knob.

She looked invitingly at Diana as if to ask whether she should keep my prick in a state of stiffness for Diana's use but Cecily took command of the situation and issued some crisp orders for us all, 'Polly, please would you keep Rupert's cock stiff for Nancy as he has yet to fulfil his promise to fuck her – as for you Henry, you should also take off your clothes and attend to the needs of young Alison who is lying there very demurely, although I can see from the lascivious look on her face that she would love to play with your circumcised cock especially as she probably hasn't seen one before.

'As for me, as Diana just said, I'm going to congratulate her in my own special way,' she added, pulling the eiderdown off the bed and spreading it on the floor next to the bed. Then she let the towel which was draped round her hips fall to the ground, and she moved across to smooth her hands sensuously over Diana's equally nude body. The two girls embraced and kissed lovingly, their tongues fluttering together as their hands roamed around the soft curves of each other's pretty rose tipped breasts. They sank down onto the eiderdown and I threw a pillow down against which Diana could rest her head as she lay back and parted her legs for Cecily's hand to insinuate itself between them.

'Oooh, what a lovely blonde pussey you have, Diana,' Cecily sighed as she cupped her hand around the exquisite blonde bush. 'Open your thighs a little wider, darling, bend your knees and then you can rub yourself off against my hand.'

Diana sighed with contentment as her delicious breasts jiggled from side to side as she worked her cunney lips backwards and forwards against the heel of Cecily's palm.

'Isn't that nice,' cooed Cecily rhetorically, as she raised her thumb to caress Diana's clitty with each upward thrusting of the blonde girl's hips. This exciting sensation made Diana moan petulantly and work her bottom faster whilst Cecily increased the pressure by cleverly swirling her thumb around the little unhooded ball which had popped out like a tiny prick from Diana's pussey.

Cecily muttered, 'Ah, darling, you have such a sensitive clitty, I can feel it bouncing against my fingers. Now let me finger fuck you – mmm, how hot it feels inside your cunney. How it sucks in my finger so easily! If only I possessed a prick I would love to slide it in and out of your honeypot.'

The lewd girl now kissed Diana's erect red nipples which had flared up into two hard little points and then swept downwards towards her sopping crack where she slid her tongue through the pouting lips deep into the cleft, prodding her clitty as she worked her tongue deeper and deeper into Diana's soaking quim, which was now creamed liberally with the pungent love juice which was running down her thighs.

Cecily's glorious young backside was now high in the air and at Polly's whispered instruction, Alison clasped hold of Henry's cock, which she had been licking and lapping up to a huge erection, and pulled my friend by his prick behind Cecily. When she saw him, she pulled her bum cheeks apart and slightly parted her legs and gasped, 'Don't go up my bum because Rupert's been there already, but you can fuck me doggie-style if you like.'

Cecily reached back and directed Henry's wide purple knob between her love lips as she bent down again and continued to suck on Diana's juicy cunt with renewed relish. The sight of this erotic tableau had sent my own tadger high in the air and Nancy, who had by now also thrown off her clothes, pulled me down on the bed and on her knees began lustily sucking my shaft, taking great gulps of cock as her head bobbed up and down, whilst Polly slid her hand between Nancy's legs and started to tickle her pussey. This so fired Alison that she lay beside me playing with her breasts whilst Nancy stretched out a hand to frig the young girl's gorgeous golden haired cunt.

I was lying on the edge of the bed and so could look down on what was happening down on the eiderdown. It was easy to tell from Diana's high-pitched squeals that she was thoroughly enjoying being licked out by Cecily, who herself was very happy at having Henry plunge his prick inside her whilst his hands came round to play with her succulent large nipples. Indeed, just as I glanced at the lascivious trio, Henry gave a deep growl and jerked back and forth in a short, convulsive movement as he creamed Cecily's cunney with a liberal coating of frothy white jism which jetted out of his twitching tool.

'A-h-r-e! A-h-r-e! A-h-r-e!' gasped Cecily as her body was racked by a thrilling all-over orgasm. She was forced to suspend her tonguing of Diana's cunt and roll out from between her legs which made the poor girl wail, 'Oh no, I haven't come yet! Henry, will you please finish me off?'

'I'll do my level best,' said Henry, taking his glistening semi-hard shaft in his hand and rubbing it furiously until it swelled back up to its fullest height.

Diana clambered up and with a gleam in her blue eyes, grasped hold of Henry's circumcised cock, 'You really must be a little tired after fucking Cecily. Lie back on this pillow and shut your eyes whilst I sit on your nice wet cock which you'll feel become embedded in my tight little wet cunney.'

He was only too pleased to fall in with such a plan and, as he stretched himself out, Diana straddled Henry's heaving frame with a quick jump and sat herself down on his thick flagpole which slid effortlessly into her sopping love box. She pivoted gracefully, swivelling on his tingling tool and bouncing up and down as he moulded her superbly firm breasts with his hands, arching his back to catch her rhythm and they moved in time, their interlocking respective cock and cunney totally oblivious to everything except their joyous mutual thrusting.

By now, Nancy was more than ready to be fucked and she lifted her lips away from my cock and gently moved her fingers away from Alison's cunt. She lay back, opened her legs and lifted her bottom as I carefully pushed my gleaming knob between her yielding cunney lips. She writhed and twisted in ecstasy in answer to my urgent pumping, her legs curled around my waist. We were both so fired up that very soon she screamed, 'I'm going to spend! I'm going to spend! Give it to me, Rupert! Come deep into me! Do it! Do it!'

I pushed forward again a few more times, but on the last delicious stroke I held my throbbing tool inside her honeypot for some fifteen seconds before pulling out my shaft completely and then with one almighty shove, I thrust in one final time and spunked great gushes of sticky jism into her welcoming love channel.

Meanwhile, a loud cry from Diana proclaimed the news that Henry's thick boner had ejaculated a copious emission of manly essence inside her pussey which left poor Polly and Alison totally cockless for neither Henry nor myself were in any state to continue this sport and both of us needed time to rejuvenate our overworked pricks and balls.

But I had not credited Polly Aysgarth with the resourcefulness which she now showed, for she rummaged underneath her dress which was lying nearby and with a flourish produced a leather box which she must have brought in my bedroom with her.

'Would you be so kind as to move up and let me snuggle up to Alison?' she enquired. Naturally, Nancy and I complied with this reasonable request. Polly thanked us and slipped in besides Alison, who murmured, 'Have you brought Herr Schnickelbaum's marvellous comforter?'

'Of course I have, you silly goose, I knew it would come in useful tonight,' said Polly, climbing on top of the trembling young girl so that their two naked bodies rubbed together cheek by jowl, or more accurately in this case, nipple to nipple and pussey to pussey. Alison threw back her head and Polly began to fondle her waiting high pointed breasts, swirling the hardened nipples in her mouth, making her shiver with lustful anticipation whilst Polly now moved her hands across the girl's white, flat belly and down into the corn-coloured silky moss of hair which lightly covered the pink, pouting pussey lips, around which Polly drew tiny, hard triangles until Alison was squirming with pleasure and then dipped her finger delicately inside Alison's yielding cunney lips.

'Oh, Polly! That's simply wonderful!' she whispered, as Polly now kissed her titties and tummy and then moved down to lap at her sopping crack. Then suddenly Polly lifted her head and asked me to pass the small leather box to her.

I did so and we all looked on with added interest as Polly opened it up and with a flourish brought out a superbly formed rubber dildo of the two headed variety – moulded by Herr Schnickelbaum of Vienna, as Polly informed us afterwards, upon the elephantine organs of Baron Lothar von Obergurgel and Count Gewirtz of Galicia.

Then she also took out of the box a bottle of orange flavoured oil and liberally poured the contents over both heads of the dildo, letting the last drains run down on to Alison's pussey which she now started to kiss again but this time, pressing the dildo to the entrance of her cunt, working it in slowly until Alison gasped out that her cunney was now crammed with this imitation prick.

Polly pulled herself up until she was sitting astride Alison's thighs, fingering herself with one hand whilst with the other she continued to fuck the younger girl's sopping pussey with the rubber cock. When her own cunt was juiced up, she carefully slid the other exposed head of the dildo into her honeypot and reached forward to pull Alison closer to her so that the two tribades were pressed together, tittie to tittie, cunt to cunt. Alison wrapped her legs as tightly as she could round Polly's back, who did the same and the two girls rocked back and forth, achieving a rhythm which was sending pulses of pleasure to every nerve centre in their bodies, and as their excitement grew, their motions became more and more frenzied.

'Aaaah! Aaaah! Polly, what a wonderful fuck! Aaaah! Aaah! Don't stop, don't stop!' screamed Alison. Polly gasped, 'I won't, I won't! How scrumptious! Do it more, that's the way!' as they fucked themselves beautifully on their magical dildo which prodded through their love channels, nipping its way through the velvety grooves of their cunts as they arched their bodies in ecstasy.

'I don't think either of them are missing our

stiff cocks at all,' Henry commented, as the two girls began to shudder and their heads thrashed about as they spent together, swimming in a sea of love juice and almost swooning clean away with the ecstatic enjoyment afforded by their efforts.

Polly and Alison lay there for some moments, heaving and panting with their cunnies still pressed together by the dildo, of which only a fraction of an inch was visible. Nancy used her long tapering fingers to manipulate it out of them, first from Alison's squelchy love channel and then from Polly's well-oiled pussey.

Watching this sensual display had excited me so much that my prick had forgotten how tired it had been and was now as hard and stiff as it had been when I had woken up back in Bedford Square at seven o'clock that morning. 'It's time to pay homage to your lovely cunt, Nancy,' I said forcefully, giving my shaft a few quick rubs to bring it up to its fullest dimensions.

'Come on then, you big cocked boy, show me what you can do!' enthused the American girl who opened her thighs as I rolled across on top of her. My hands moved over her aroused body with practised ease. I squeezed her large, firm breasts and rubbed the big, dark nipples against my palms which made them rise up into little red stalks. I kissed her forehead and worked downwards via her cheeks, lips, breasts and tummy to her open, wet cunney which smelled really nice, with a spicy tang that had my mouth watering. I slurped around Nancy's cunt and prised open her pussey lips with my fingers, sinking them slowly into her sopping slit which was already dribbling with love juice. She squeezed her breasts as I gently heaved myself upwards and when I was on top of her she wrapped her arms and legs around me as I guided my cock into her glistening little nookie and at once we fell into a completely abandoned bout of wild, uninhibited fucking.

Nancy managed to contract her cunney muscles so that her honeypot took hold of my prick like a delicate, soft hand as I pumped my raging shaft in and out of her sodden pussey. She urged me to thrust deeper as she raised her legs to rest them on my shoulders and her juices dripped against my balls as they banged against her arse. Cupped now in my palms, her tight bum cheeks rotated almost savagely as my lusty cock drove home, and her kisses rained upon my neck as the friction in her love channel reached new heights and the sensual girl reached climax after climax as my throbbing tool slewed back and forth.

'Go on, Rupert, spunk into me,' she gasped, and I plunged down as hard as I could, crushing her luscious breasts beneath me as her cunt squeezed my cock even more tightly and this voluptuous pressure was too great for me to bear. I sensed the creamy jism rising from my balls and seconds later, with a tremendous woosh, it surged out of me, spurting from my knob inside her in a huge spend which seemed to last and last as I ejaculated what seemed like gallons of sticky spunk into Nancy's juicy, dark warmth, whilst she gripped my bottom and pushed me ever deeper inside her as we shouted with joy in our mutual orgasm.

She squeezed my balls as I withdrew and the last drains of my emission trickled down her thigh as we lay back exhausted though we had enough energy to raise a smile when our audience spontaneously broke into a round of applause.

'That was a very well-executed fuck, if I might be so bold as to say so,' commented Polly, and Diana agreed, saying, 'There's a lot to be said for the good old-fashioned missionary position.'

'Very true,' said Cecily thoughtfully. 'Although I am very fond of the Eastern position much favoured by Sir Clive Bull where the man sits down with his feet crossed and you sit on his cock with your feet round his back. You only have to rock backwards and forwards for your clitty to be wonderfully stimulated.'

Diana nodded her head and said, 'I'm also keen on that position, especially with such a thick prick as Sir Clive's in my cunt, but have you tried the Lotus variation which I think is even better? One of my lecturers at the Sorbonne taught this to me – the boy lies supine whilst you sit on top of him with your back turned to his face whilst you fold your legs into the classic Oriental position with each foot placed on the opposite thigh. His cock enters you from the rear which I always enjoy and uses his arms to steady you. I just close my eyes and lose myself in self absorbed contemplation as I bounce up and down on his throbbing cock.'

'I've never tried fucking that way,' said Alison shyly, 'but then I do like to thresh around and grab hold of my boy friend's cock and play with his balls whilst we are fucking, just like you did, Miss Diana, with Mr Henry's prick.'

'Well, I must say that I do prefer looking at my partner,' declared Henry, as Diana gave his prick a few loving rubs and it rose majestically to attention from the curly black mass of hair at the base of his belly, 'otherwise the whole act becomes too impersonal for my liking, and as far as I'm concerned, the cleft position for fucking takes a lot of beating as it allows you to look at each other although there is a degree of detachment for either party if they want it.

'It's not difficult to get into either – this is how I love to do it. I kneel, leaning backwards from the waist with my left hand behind me on the bed for support. The girl sits astride in basically the same position with her arms extended behind her. We're able to look at one another but from some way away as we both now lean backwards. However, as she's sitting on my thighs above me with only my hand on her backside, it's up to her to control the pace of the fuck.'

This little lecture seemed to spur Diana who bent down in front of Henry as she frigged his sinewy shaft and then opened her lips and took his hairy ballsack into her mouth, sucking slowly first one ball and then the other. The sight of this erotic play stirred my own prick which swelled up to attention as I jumped off the bed, positioned myself behind Diana's delicious bum cheeks, and pulled aside the soft globes to edge my knob towards her pouting cunt.

She reached behind for my cock and guided my

tool towards its chosen port of call and with one vigorous shove I buried my shaft in to the hilt and my balls flopped against her heaving bum cheeks. This scene so excited Cecily that she slid herself between my legs and began to copy what Diana was doing to Henry, licking and lapping my balls and gobbling them each in turn inside her wet mouth and coating them with her saliva from her wet tongue.

I thrust my cock back and forth as I flicked my fingers around Diana's hard, red nipples in an ecstasy of enjoyment and the other girls now joined this stimulating fucking chain by joining Nancy on the bed. Whilst Diana continued to frig his cock and suck his balls, Henry took the dildo in his hand and leaning forward, slid it into Polly's waiting honeypot whilst the lewd girl, who was lying between Nancy and Alison, used her hands to finger fuck each of the other girls' pussies whilst they sucked her titties. Henry and I changed positions to ensure that every girl was afforded the pleasure of having a thick throbbing length of prick in their cunney and we manfully managed to give each of them satisfaction before we all collapsed into a sweaty, naked heap of bodies on my bed.

However, at around two o'clock in the morning I woke up with a start. It suddenly occurred to me that what now seemed ages ago before our lustful orgy, Cecily and I had left my parents, Aunt Penelope and the Wigmores to their bridge and had not returned even to say good-night! I gnawed on my bottom lip as I wondered whether the others had also rushed up to my room without going back to see the older members of the household.

Polly stirred and asked what was the matter, but when I told her she whispered, 'Don't worry, Rupert, your Aunt Penelope is a real sport. She guessed what was going to happen tonight and before Alison and I came up here, your Aunt told me that she would make apologies on your behalf and tell your parents that the young guests were all rather tired and had gone upstairs for an early night. She knew the others wouldn't mind as they were all keen bridge players which let her off the hook and she was also able to slip away upstairs for a nice fuck.'

'Three cheers for Aunt Penelope! But what are you talking about her slipping away for a nice fuck?'

'Oh dear, I'm sorry, I shouldn't have said anything, Mister Rupert, but I thought you knew about your Aunt and Mr Goldhill,' she said apologetically.

'Goldhill?' I echoed blankly. 'Are you telling me that our butler has been fucking my Aunt?'

'Well, yes, I'm surprised you never knew. I've a shrewd suspicion that your mother has guessed what's been going on over the last couple of years.'

She yawned and snuggled back down against the small of Henry's back. 'Come on, let's get back to sleep,' she muttered, but my curiosity was aroused. I slipped out of bed, put on a dressing gown and tip-toed upstairs to the servants' quarters. Was old Goldhill really slewing his gnarled old truncheon in and out of my Aunt's juicy pussey? I scoffed at the thought, but seeing is believing. When silently I opened his bedroom door, with my own eyes I saw our faithful old retainer and Aunt Penelope together in each other's arms, with her hand clasped round his cock even though they were both fast asleep.

I closed the door as silently as I had opened it and made my way back to my own room. At first I was irritated by the fact that our servant had fucked an honorary member of the Mountjoy family but I soon came to realise that this was an unworthy thought. After all, Aunt Penelope must have wanted the liaison, so in fact our butler had only been doing his duty! Why, it would serve Uncle Stephen right for leaving her alone so often – I remember my mother saying once that she was certain that he could cut down his trips to our capital city if he so wished. 'I can't think why he wants to go to London so often,' she had said to my father, 'and why doesn't he ever take Penelope with him? For instance, he only went to a meeting at his club last week.'

As my more radical female friends are wont to say these days, what's sauce for the goose is sauce for the gander, which would explain why even if she had guessed what was going on, my mother had decided that it served Stephen right if his wife was forced to look elsewhere for her intimate needs.

With that in mind, I settled down to go back to sleep. But Polly had other ideas and she grabbed hold of my prick as soon as I returned to bed. 'Now you've woken me up, I can't get back to sleep,' she complained, stroking my shaft so sensuously that it immediately swelled and bounded in her hand.

'Polly, you've got to be up at six o'clock as usual,' I warned her but she pouted her lips and continued to frig my cock and begged me to thread her juicy cunney. 'It's my day off tomorrow so I'd love a quick little fuck,' she pleaded as she kissed my uncapped knob, 'then I'll be able to fall asleep.'

Well, how caddish it would be to refuse a request from a damsel in distress? I followed her as she slipped out of bed and lay on the carpet, leaning back and raising her knees, spreading them invitingly as I moved across her and planted her legs on top of my shoulders.

'We must be quiet and not disturb the others,' I said softly as I rubbed the tip of my cock against her soaking crack and slowly sank my shaft inside her wet cunt. I pulled out and re-entered, and her slick love channel clasped my cock lovingly with each long, slow stroke. Although this was as enjoyable as ever, the hour was too late for a prolonged bout and as soon as my balls began rhythmically to slap against her backside, I let myself go and unleashed a flood of hot spunk inside her luscious love nest which caused her to shiver all over and spend profusely. Polly was as good as her word for almost as soon as we had climbed back into bed, she snuggled down again and was asleep within minutes.

But I lay awake for a while musing on the morrow. This coming day we were all travelling to York for the evening reception for His Gracious Majesty King Edward VII. I was looking forward to meeting the Merry Monarch who was, from all accounts, a man after my own heart, who enjoyed life to the full. I would go to York with a sore cock after this wild night's fucking, which was not yet over, for the girls would doubtless demand that Henry and I perform again when they woke up. But I would also have a light heart as the main mission – to help Diana Wigmore's career progress – had been accomplished and brewing in the back of my mind was a happy intuition that in the next few days I would be taking part in some further lusty bedroom adventures.

Was I to be proved right? I will tell all, dear reader, in frank, uncensored detail, in the next volume of my memoirs.

TO BE CONTINUED . . .